Whit Spun On
Out Of The Ro
Dropped Her

The ever-present tears welled up again and splashed down her cheeks.

Six more weeks.

The countdown preyed on her mind, spoiling her pleasure in every waking minute of the day. But she had no right to be angry with Whit. He'd been patient and kind, doing everything possible to make life easier for her.

If only he could—

No! A thousand times a day she caught herself wishing for the moon. She'd gone out of her way to let him know she was attracted to him, and that she loved the island, too. He probably knew she was in love with him. If he wanted her, he'd have said so by now.

And she couldn't change that. In six weeks, she'd be walking away from Whit Montgomery forever.

Whit, *and* their baby.

Dear Reader,

Welcome to March! Spring is in the air. The birds are chirping, the bees are buzzing . . . and men and women all over the world are thinking about—love.

Here at Silhouette Desire we take love *very* seriously. We're committed to bringing you six terrific stories all about love each and every month of the year, and this March is no exception.

Let's start with March's *Man of the Month* by Jackie Merritt. It's called *Tennessee Waltz,* and I know you're going to love this story. Next, Naomi Horton returns with *Chastity's Pirate.* (How can you resist a book with a title like this? You just *can't!*) And look for books by Anne Marie Winston, Barbara McCauley, Justine Davis and new-to-Desire Kat Adams.

And in months to come, some of your very favorite authors are coming your way. Look for sensuous romances from the talented pens of Dixie Browning, Lass Small, Cait London, Barbara Boswell . . . just to name a few.

So go wild with Desire, and start thinking about love.

All the best,

Lucia Macro
Senior Editor

ANNE MARIE WINSTON

ISLAND BABY

SILHOUETTE *Desire*®

Published by Silhouette Books New York

America's Publisher of Contemporary Romance

SILHOUETTE BOOKS
300 East 42nd St., New York, N.Y. 10017

ISLAND BABY

ISBN: 0-373-05770-9

First Silhouette Books printing March 1993

Printed in the U.S.A.

Books by Anne Marie Winston

Silhouette Desire

Best Kept Secrets #742
Island Baby #770

ANNE MARIE WINSTON

began her writing career at the age of nine, when she penned a weekly newspaper, conned her mother into typing it and then badgered all the neighbors to pay a nickel per copy. Always an insatiable reader, she resisted her college roommate's suggestion that she write a novel of her own, until nearly a decade later.

A former educator and strong advocate of literacy programs, Anne Marie has acted, danced and choreographed nonprofessionally. She will do anything—almost—for chocolate, enjoys philately and needlework, tolerates aerobics and golfs enough to please her husband. They share a southern Pennsylvania home with two daughters, two cats and a collie.

With special thanks to:
Dr. James I. Richardson, PhD,
Director of the Georgia Sea Turtle Cooperative
at the University of Georgia, Athens,
who made time for me during his "busy season"
on Little Cumberland Island
and
who is doing a superb job trying to save the turtles.

One

———

"What I need is a surrogate mother." Sunlight washed over Whit Montgomery as he pushed out of the leather chair in his lawyer's office. Stopping at the window, he stared down at the sea smashing against the Georgia coastline. Even in early December it was enticing, emerald whitecaps dancing in the mild breeze. How could he ever live away from the sea?

"What you need is a mercenary bitch with no maternal instincts whatsoever."

"Exactly." Whit was sadly afraid Ira Hanrahan was right. And if he couldn't find such a woman, his dreams would be on the auctioneer's block, along with his ancestral home at the start of the new year. He turned and pinned the older man with a direct stare. "Got anyone in mind?"

Ira shook his head. He ran a distracted hand through his elegantly styled silver hair. "I'm afraid you're hunting an illusion," he said with a wry grimace. "I've never met a woman as hard-boiled as that. Now let me get this again.

You want to find a woman to be a surrogate mother. One
who would bear you a child for a sum specified in contrac-
tual agreement, one who would relinquish all claim to said
child after the birth.''

"Right."

"Jeez." Ira sighed. "Wouldn't it be easier to get married? What are you going to do with a baby out there on that
island?"

Whit turned his back on the sea and plunged his hands
into the pockets of his navy dress pants. He snorted, mock-
ing himself. "No, it would *not* be easier to get married. You
know how long my mother lasted on the island. And my one
attempt at marriage didn't even make it to the altar when she
found out I wasn't planning to move to the mainland.
Women need more social life than the turtles and I can provide." His voice dropped as he struggled with remembered
rejection. Once he'd dreamed of a woman who'd love his
untouched island home, and of the children they'd raise together. Now he knew better. "Are you sure Granddad's will
is legal?"

"It's legal, all right. I wrote that will, remember?"

"I remember." Whit knew a surprising sense of relief. He
caught the smile that threatened so his lawyer wouldn't think
he'd lost his mind. "I've given this a lot of thought, Ira. The
chance to have a child of my own is exciting. After the first
few years, I'll be able to share the turtles with him, pass on
my work to someone who'll love it like I do."

"It might be a 'her,' you know."

Whit shrugged. "I'm no chauvinist. A girl would be fine.
A girl who was brought up on the island would be able to
handle the isolation. It would be very different from trans-
planting a full-grown woman who's already accustomed to
another life-style."

"And you still insist on those unusual terms?"

"Yes." Whit was decisive. "When you're looking for a
candidate, be sure you inform them of the conditions. I'm
willing to pay a significant fee for in vitro fertilization, but

the balance will have to be paid after the birth of the child. If the lady insists on going the old-fashioned route—''

"Intercourse," supplied Ira with a grin.

"Yeah. I'll pay up front as soon as the pregnancy is confirmed, but the fee will be somewhat less than if she agrees to in vitro."

"I don't get it. You're offering more money for the in vitro process, but she has to wait to get it?"

Whit shrugged defensively. "It makes sense to me. I'm not wealthy, at least not until the estate is settled. I can't pay for the in vitro procedure *and* remunerate the woman all at once. If the surrogate chooses in vitro, she'll have to wait until after the baby comes for the rest of the money, so I have to sweeten the pot to make that option worthwhile."

"I still don't understand why you don't offer the same amount for the end result, regardless of the means."

"I consider in vitro fertilization the best option." Whit could feel his face heating.

Ira smirked. "This could be interesting. What if we get some kinky broad who insists on a face-to-face encounter?"

"I'm depending on you to avoid that. Besides, any woman who'd consider this at all is going to want all the money she can get her hands on. I'm betting you'll find someone willing to wait for a big, fat check." Whit glared at Ira, embarrassed and irritated by his friend's amusement. "Believe me, I don't want to act as a stud service."

Ira laughed. "I see your point. Spontaneity, where art thou?" Then he sobered. "I still think this is one of the worst ideas you've ever had."

"Fine." Whit stalked over and slapped his large, scarred hands onto the top of Ira's desk in exasperation. "*You* tell *me* how else I can meet the terms of the will without entering into a marriage." He held up a warning finger as Ira tried to speak. "Which I absolutely will not consider."

Ira leaned back as far as his comfortable chair permitted.

"Well, hell," he said finally. "There's no other way. Your grandfather figured he'd outsmart you with this maneuver. Adoption wouldn't satisfy him. Robert wanted to make sure the land gets passed down to his grandchild someday, and if you wouldn't do it by choice, he thought he could force you into it."

"He succeeded." Whit spun away from the desk and moved over to contemplate the soothing view out the window again. His options were limited and he knew it. If he didn't produce an heir within a year, his family's two hundred-year-old estate on Turtle Island just off the coast of southern Georgia would be sold at public auction. And it would be his fault. "The federal government's endangered habitats program has already overextended their budget—I checked. If that land goes public, there's no way I can afford to purchase it. And developers would be able to top any price wildlife conservation groups could scrape up."

"You're right." Ira's tone wasn't encouraging. "The only way Turtle Island's going to remain undeveloped is if you're able to keep it in the family."

"There won't *be* a family unless you come up with a suitable candidate." *Family.* The word had a nice ring. He'd all but given up the dream of a child of his own until the stipulations in his grandfather's will had started the wheels turning in his head. He'd never realized how much fatherhood meant to him until the opportunity presented itself without the added complication of a woman who would demand that he move away from the work and the life he loved.

"All right. I'll look into it." Ira came around the desk and offered his hand to Whit. "I'm sorry about this mess. Ol' Robert wouldn't hear of any other terms—believe me, I tried."

Whit shook the proffered hand firmly before turning toward the door. "I know, Ira." He smiled fondly. "He was a stubborn old mule, wasn't he? Well, thanks for your time. I guess I'll wait to hear from you on this." He ran a finger around the starched collar of his white shirt, then yanked loose the knot of the tie. Ah, relief. He couldn't wait to get out of these clothes. "The sooner the better."

Twisting the polished knob of Ira's light oak office door, Whit strode through the outer office. The receptionist looked up and smiled as he passed. Whit nodded and returned the smile; she hadn't been there when he and Ira had come in from their lunch meeting to continue their discussion.

Too bad he couldn't find a woman who looked like her to be the mother of his child. She was a beauty—wavy ash-blond hair and enormous violet eyes set in a small heart-shaped face. The trim figure he could see above the desk was gently rounded. He bet she had great legs.

He thought about asking her out, but as always, his feet carried him past her and out into the hallway before he could act on the notion. What was the point in dating when bitter experience had taught him no sane woman would ever consider living his life-style? He'd be stupid to try to date now, anyway. With any luck at all, he'd be a father within the year.

"Susannah? We're ready for you to join us now." Ira stuck his head out of his office and motioned to her.

Susannah Taylor slowly got to her feet. Her stomach was tied in knots of apprehension as she moved toward the inevitable confrontation in Ira's office. *The interview.*

A lock of ash-blond hair fell forward over one shoulder and she carefully pushed it back. She needed to look calm and controlled, despite the way her legs were trembling. It was vital that she present her best appearance.

When she reached the door, Ira clasped her elbow. "Are you sure you want to do this? I wish you'd reconsider."

Susannah gathered her composure, looking up at her concerned employer. "I don't have a choice. Becca will die without that operation, and you know I can't ask Steve for money."

"You *won't* ask Steve," Ira shot back in a furious undertone. "I still think we could get the bastard for desertion and failure to provide child support."

"Perhaps." Susannah's whisper was equally fierce. "But by the time we did, Becca would be dead. I don't care if Steve Taylor drops off the face of the earth tomorrow, but I won't lose my daughter."

Ira held up his hands defensively, accepting defeat. "Okay. Are you ready to meet Mr. Montgomery?"

She nodded and preceded Ira into the office.

"Whit, this is my receptionist, Susannah Taylor."

The man in the leather chair rose and turned toward her as Ira completed the introduction. "Susannah, Robert Whittier Montgomery the Fifth."

"Whit. Please call me Whit." The man extended his hand as she studied him.

She recognized him from his last visit to the office, of course. He wasn't a man any woman could easily ignore. He had…sex appeal. He was much taller than her own five foot two, perhaps close to six feet. Sable hair so dark that it appeared black displayed marvelous mink shades as she drew closer. His eyes were a surprising deep, deep blue. Becca's eyes had been that exact intense shade when she was a newborn, but Susannah had never seen it on an adult before. They were fringed by thick, dark lashes the same shade as his hair. He wasn't handsome, exactly, with that squared-off jaw, blunt, high cheekbones and an oddly bent nose that looked as if he'd lost a round with a boxer. But as Susannah cataloged his looks, she was conscious of his appeal. Maybe it stemmed from the gentleness in those striking eyes.

His hand closed gently over her palm and she started at the surge of heat the sensation produced within her. Abruptly she became aware that he was still holding her hand and she was gawking at him like a smitten teenager. *Oh, good, Susannah, very good. You have to impress this guy, remember?*

Withdrawing her hand, she murmured a conventional greeting. "It's a pleasure to meet you, Whit." But it wasn't. Not when she thought about what she was going to do for this man.

She chose a seat and turned toward Ira expectantly. Her employer gave her a reassuring smile before he said, "I think you two should discuss this privately. I'll be right outside if you need anything." He left the office before she could protest.

When the door clicked behind him, the silence in the room was a palpable presence. Whit was still standing by the desk. Susannah fought a wave of self-consciousness. How did one start to discuss something like this?

Finally, when she made no move to speak, he began. "Uh, Ira tells me you're agreeable to the terms of the contract."

"Yes." Susannah confirmed his words quietly. She hoped he hadn't seen her nervous swallow.

The warmth in his eyes disappeared and his face seemed to harden slightly as he looked directly at her. "You're willing to bear a child for me, Ms. Taylor?"

"Missus," she corrected automatically. "Yes, I am."

"Why?"

She took a deep breath. "My reasons are private, but I assure you I am willing to sign anything you require."

"You'd give up a child? Never make any attempt to see it?"

Susannah met his eyes. "Yes. Ira has already shared with you my stipulations. A written report of progress every three months for the first two years, then once a year after that, including medical and educational records as they become available. I would need to be satisfied that a child I bore was being given love and attention."

Did she imagine it or did those blue eyes soften a bit?

"Mrs. Taylor, I want a baby. It will be loved."

"Mr. Montgomery, may I ask you a personal question?"

"Whit. Go ahead." He nodded encouragingly.

"Why don't you just get married? Surely you've met women—"

"My circumstances are rather unique, Mrs. Taylor. I live on an island. I don't socialize much. Not too many women are willing to endure that kind of isolation for long." His voice was brusque. It suggested that she'd be well advised to restrain any more personal curiosity.

"Well . . ." She couldn't think of another thing to say.

"I may as well call Ira back in here and he can start the paperwork." Whit made a beeline for the door.

Why, he's as nervous as I am, Susannah realized.

Ira reentered the room, clapping his hands heartily. "What's the verdict?"

"We'd like you to witness the contract," Whit said quietly.

Some of the merriment faded from Ira's face. "I have one right here. All you have to do is specify which version of the contract you wish. We can get the legal work done today and set up an appointment for Susannah at the hospital in Atlanta."

"I won't need an appointment." Susannah's voice was quiet but firm. She couldn't look at either man, so she stared out the window at the wispy white clouds, concentrating on the changing patterns of shadow they cast across the surface of the sea.

Ira's voice was persuasive, as if he didn't want to acknowledge what she'd said. "Sure you will. Whit wants to set up the in vitro procedure as soon as possible."

"Ira, I can't go to Atlanta. *You know that.*" Susannah transferred her gaze to Ira, willing him to get her silent message. She couldn't leave Becca for any length of time. "Also—" she took a deep breath and faced Whit "—I'd prefer to receive remuneration early in the pregnancy."

Her words rang in the sunny office. It was so quiet she swore she could hear the waves through the soundproof glass.

"You don't want to have in vitro fertilization?" Whit's navy eyes bored holes in her as she met his stunned gaze.

"No." She let the bald negative hang in the air. She didn't owe this man any explanations, she reminded herself.

Ira dropped his pen on the desk with a loud *clack*. "Susannah, do you realize what you're saying?"

"Yes." She prayed for composure as she faced Ira again. "I need the money as soon as possible. Besides, statistically, in vitro fertilization is considerably less successful than..."

"Intercourse at the time of ovulation," Ira supplied grimly.

Susannah could feel the heat rising in her cheeks.

Whit was still staring at her as if he couldn't believe what he was hearing, but finally he came to her aid. "Whatever the lady prefers is fine. Let's sign the papers." As Ira shrugged helplessly and picked up his pen again, Whit addressed her. "How will you know—how will I know—?"

Susannah realized what he was mumbling about, and her practical side took over. If she just didn't think about this happening to *her,* she could handle it. "I'll take my basal temperature and have Ira call you when the time is right. I did that with my first child so I hope it will be as easy to conceive this time. I suspect I'll ovulate in about three weeks."

Whit's face was expressionless. "All right."

Ira knew when he was defeated. Quickly he prepared the necessary documents. Susannah hesitated only a moment when the cold metal of Ira's expensive pen was pressed into her hand.

This contract would give her the means to save her daughter's life, to survive the expenses that accompanied open-heart surgery. With the money from this, she could give the surgeons the go-ahead to set a date to operate.

She'd miss the baby every day for the rest of her life, but Becca would be alive. That thought gave her the impetus to set the pen to the paper and sign her name in a beautifully rounded script. With determination born of desperation, she pushed away the pain that hovered.

As Susannah pushed the completed papers back across the desk to Ira, she noticed Whit drawing out his wallet. Extracting a check, he extended it to her. "Here's the first installment as specified in the contract. Another sum will be paid at the time your pregnancy is medically confirmed."

Susannah twisted her fingers together. "That's okay. You can pay it all in one lump sum." She resisted the urge to put her hands behind her back.

"No, I insist. I'd prefer to stick to the bargain." Whit reached for her hand and pressed the check into her palm.

Again she was aware of the surprising heat that radiated from his skin. Her fingers closed over the check reflexively and immediately he withdrew his hand.

"I'll, uh, see you in a couple of weeks, then," he said.

She nodded. Rising from the chair, she slipped out of the room. Behind her, she could hear Ira saying, "Stick around for a few minutes, Whit. I'd like to talk to you."

Three weeks later Susannah lay in bed. It was early, but she was already awake, taking her temperature as the method of determining ovulation demanded. She was roused from morose contemplation of the basal thermometer by a childish voice.

"Mom-mee! Mom-mee! I go see? San'a come, Mom-mee?"

Her own concerns were swept aside as memory washed over her in a trice. Christmas morning! This was Becca's first real Christmas. Last year she'd been barely a year old, far too young to comprehend the magic of the season. Throwing back the covers, she crossed the small bedroom to Becca's crib.

The little girl was standing with her beloved blanket clutched in one fist. As she saw Susannah approach, she squealed and bounced up and down on short legs. "San'a come, Mom-mee!"

"Yes, Becca, I think Santa Claus came last night." Susannah's voice reflected the love she felt for this tiny miracle. "Let's change your diaper, then we'll go see what Santa left for you."

She cuddled the toddler close for a minute, then competently fastened a clean diaper into place before setting the child on the floor.

"Too-ees, Mom-mee?"

"Yes, I bet he left toys for you. Were you a good girl?"

"Uh-*huh!*"

"Okay. Let's go look under the tree." Susannah followed as Becca's churning legs pounded out of the room and down the short hallway to the living room where they'd decorated a small tree with popcorn and paper chains.

As trees went, it was a pretty pitiful effort, but Becca seemed delighted with it. She was too young to comprehend the difference between her tree and the lavish displays in the store windows they'd passed.

Thank God. She was too young to comprehend a lot of things. If everything worked out, she'd never have to know her mother sold a baby to pay for her life.

If. What a frightening word. Susannah had found herself praying a lot lately. So much could go wrong during surgery, and the surgeon had already explained the risks involved in correcting a heart defect such as the one Becca had been born with two years ago.

Several hours after breakfast, Susannah left Becca playing happily on the floor with a new teddy bear then padded into the tiny kitchen and reached for the telephone. Dialing Ira's number, she counted the rings and prayed he was home.

"Hello?"

"Ira, it's Susannah."

"Merry Christmas!" Immediately his voice changed. "Is Rebecca all right?"

Warmed by his concern for her daughter, she hastened to reassure him. "Becca's fine. She's in the living room exploring her new toys right now. I'm sorry to bother you on Christmas morning, but . . . this is the time." When he remained silent, she continued. "You know, the time for . . . it's the right time . . . to call Whit," she finally managed.

"Oh, right." Ira was abruptly all business. "You mean tonight?"

"It'll have to be tonight unless he wants to wait till next month." Even though Ira was on the other end of a telephone, she could feel a blush creeping up her cheeks.

"Can you get a sitter that quick?"

"Yes. My next-door neighbor will keep Becca."

"Okay. Will do. I'll get back to you after I talk to him."

"Thanks, Ira. And Merry Christmas."

Hanging up the receiver with relief, Susannah returned to the living room. Becca grabbed a new storybook off the floor, where she'd been amusing herself by making necklaces out of the bright ribbons strewn everywhere. " 'Tory, Mom-mee."

Seizing the opportunity to get her mind off the ordeal ahead of her, she said, "Okay, baby, I'll read you a story."

She settled Becca's slight weight in her lap and began to read. Within minutes, the fair head began to droop and Susannah realized that the little girl was sound asleep.

She carried Becca into the bedroom they shared. Placing her in the crib, she covered her with a light quilt. One of the side effects of the illness Becca suffered from was chronic exhaustion. The child took as many as three long naps a day at a time when most toddlers were down to one.

Her heart lightened as she thought that within just a few weeks, she might be able to schedule Becca's surgery. Then she could lead a more normal life. Becca was quick as a whip now. With more energy she'd be unstoppable.

Susannah showered and dressed. She was cleaning up the remains of Becca's Christmas when the telephone rang. Ira.

"Hello?"

"Hello, Mrs. Taylor. This is Whit Montgomery. I asked Ira if I could call you. I thought it would be easier if we work out the details between us."

Susannah's relief at not having to endure Ira's silent disapproval made her reply heartfelt. "Thank you."

When she said nothing further, Whit went on. "How about if I pick you up at seven and we go out for dinner? We can go dancing after that and see how things go. I want you to feel comfortable about this."

"That sounds . . . nice."

"I've reserved a suite at the hotel where I made the dinner reservations. If you'd like to bring an overnight case, we can have it sent up when we arrive."

He'd thought of everything. "Thank you," she said again.

"Certainly. I'll see you at seven." After getting her address, he hung up.

Susannah stared into space. He'd been very thoughtful. He wouldn't have had to treat this like a date and he most certainly didn't have to concern himself with her comfort.

A warm inner glow suffused her. He seemed to be a nice man.

Taking advantage of Becca's nap, Susannah trekked across the hall and knocked on Myrna Rowan's door. The widow kept Becca during the day while Susannah worked. She'd been shocked to learn of the little girl's life-threatening condition, but in practical Myrna fashion, she'd prepared herself to handle anything. Susannah couldn't have felt safer if she were home with Becca every minute of the day.

After she confirmed the arrangements with Myrna, Susannah returned to her apartment. Becca's lisping treble came floating out of the bedroom. "Mom-mee? Up now." It wasn't a question.

Listening with half an ear to Becca's incessant commentary as she examined her new toys, Susannah wandered across the room to the bookshelf where pictures of Becca graced every available surface. She picked up one of Becca at four months, toothless and bald, grinning at something the photographer had been waving just out of range. It was one of Susannah's favorites.

Setting it down, she traced a finger over another one, of Becca in the bathtub without a stitch of clothing on. She was about eight months in that one.

Her finger shook as she realized that she'd never have pictures like this of the child she was contracted to give to Whit Montgomery. She bowed her head against the bookshelf, clutching one of the shelves so hard her fingertips hurt.

It's the only way. She repeated the thought over and over again, taking deep, calming breaths until she could force back the tears that threatened. She'd be sure this child was well and happy, and Becca would live. That was what she had to focus on. *Becca would live.*

Two

Whit climbed out of the Mercedes his grandfather had kept on the mainland. Squinting up at the three-story brick apartments in front of him, he wondered again why Susannah Taylor needed money so badly she couldn't wait nine months. Maybe she was a compulsive gambler and had gotten herself in too deep. Or perhaps she was a credit-card crazy, someone who couldn't manage to equate what was spent on a little piece of plastic with the actual sum that was due at the end of the month. Either reason seemed a poor excuse to sell a child.

He reminded himself not to be judgmental. Mrs. Taylor's reasons, whatever they were, would give him the child he was beginning to anticipate already with almost painful intensity.

He was curious about what he'd find inside Mrs. Taylor's home. From the looks of her choice of housing, she wasn't living in luxury. As apartments went, this place was nothing great, but it looked clean and neat and in good condition. In several of the residents' windows, he could see Christmas trees with their lights winking merrily.

Christmas. It hadn't meant much to him in recent years. Granddad had liked to decorate the house, but there was no wonder, no mystery to it anymore. If this night produced the desired results, he'd be worrying about tree trimmings and gifts and visits to Santa Claus for quite a few years to come.

The thought of what was to happen in the immediate future stuck with him as he mounted the steps. Susannah Taylor wasn't hard to look at. That piquant face captured a man's eye and her slim figure was just curvy enough to make him drool. Her legs were every bit as spectacular as he'd imagined they'd be that first day he'd noticed her in Ira's office.

He'd been stunned when Ira escorted the pretty receptionist through the door for the surrogate interview. Days earlier, he'd read the thick file of information Ira had compiled for him. He knew the applicant was divorced and the mother of one daughter. He'd also checked out the medical history information carefully, but he'd never given a thought to what the woman might look like. When the blonde with striking violet eyes had walked into the room, he'd been knocked for a loop.

That was when he'd assumed she'd want in vitro fertilization. He was ashamed to admit, even to himself, that his body had leaped to attention like an eagle who'd spotted a hare when he'd understood what she meant with her prim little phrase. *I'd prefer to receive remuneration when the pregnancy is confirmed.* He knew Ira had explained the terms to her—she knew she was agreeing to have intercourse with him.

Of course, some of his reaction might have been caused by his self-imposed abstention in recent years. He hadn't seen many women, anyway, and the ones he had seen just didn't appeal somehow. Not the way Susannah did.

Locating the main door to the apartments, he entered a foyer. The residents' names were listed discreetly beside mailboxes. Ascending the inside stairs, he walked down the hallway until he came to 3-C and knocked. Susannah opened the door right away.

"Merry Christmas." She greeted him with a determined smile. "I'll be ready to go as soon as I take my daughter across the hall to her baby-sitter. Make yourself at home."

Whit merely nodded. He'd probably babble if he tried to speak right now anyway. He'd thought she was pretty before, but tonight she was gorgeous. As he surveyed her, he wondered how in the world any man had let her get away. The dress was simple, he supposed by some standards, hugging her body from the scooped neck to her knees. It was some fuzzy fabric... velvet? The deep, almost-black violet enhanced her eyes and emphasized her fair skin. When she turned to cross the room, his heartbeat jumped about two speeds faster.

Who said this dress was simple? Although it met at the neck, the material was cut in a sort of keyhole that showed an incredible amount of creamy skin that stretched from her nape to the back of her waist. And her smooth, stockinged legs were enough to drive him crazy. He shifted uncomfortably on the sofa he'd chosen. His body had been revved all day, preparing in its own way for tonight's... task. Seeing Susannah in that dress was definitely putting a strain on his good intentions, not to mention the expensive wool pants he wore.

She disappeared from view and he expelled a sigh of relief. Curiously he scrutinized her home. A mishmash of well-worn furniture and children's toys was the most noticeable decor. An afghan and several pillows in shades of blue lent a cozy air to the room. A few pictures of a baby hung on one wall and more were scattered over the large bookcase at one end of the living area. The windows wore slatted blinds but no curtains. She'd hung several lush potted plants in them to soften the look. In one corner, a small evergreen had been festively dressed in homemade strands of popcorn and paper, and a child's original creations hung from a few branches.

In just a moment, she returned. His eyes were riveted to the bundle she carried in her arms. Somehow, it hadn't computed when he'd read that she had a child. Let's see, it was a girl. Rebecca.

Automatically he got to his feet. "Can I see her?"

Susannah smiled. A real smile, he noted. Not that guarded look she'd given him at the door. It brightened her eyes immeasurably. "Sure. She's just waking up. My neighbor keeps her while I work and she's thrilled to have her tonight, too."

Some of the light went out of her smile and he knew she was thinking the same thing he was. *Tonight.*

He'd reached her side, and she shifted the sleepy child from her shoulder to hold her in her arms. Leaning closer, Whit saw that the little girl was a beauty. Just like her mother. Tousled blond hair and huge violet eyes. As he stared, the tot strained to be held upright in her mother's arms.

"Mom-mee fren?"

"Yes, this is my friend. Can you say 'Mr. Montgomery'?"

The child hesitated, and Whit said, "Can you say 'Whit'?"

"Whit," she repeated with obvious glee as she gave him a devilish grin.

"You're a doll," he said. "Can I hold you?" He held out his arms and to his delight, she came right to him. As he lifted her close, his arm brushed against Susannah's breast. He wondered if she felt the same shock of heat that went through him every time they touched. He'd noticed it in Ira's office weeks ago when he'd taken her hand. "What's your name?"

"Bec-ca." The little girl sounded as if she had a mouthful of marbles, but he didn't care.

"She talks well," he told Susannah.

A fond maternal smile touched her lips. "I think so. She was just two on the first of the month."

Becca put her hands on either side of his face, directing his attention back to her. "Whit Bec-ca's fren?"

"Yes, honey, I'd love to be your friend," he said gravely. God, she was precious. And she felt like a feather in his arms. He'd never been around small children much. Suddenly it hit him that *his* child might look very much like this. The wonder of it made him swallow. He could hardly wait!

"If you'd like to carry her, we'll just drop her next door on our way out," Susannah said. She led the way out of the apartment, pausing to lock the door. He noticed that she set a small overnight bag discreetly out of sight before she knocked on the door of 3-B.

The door opened before Susannah had finished knocking.

"There's my little sweetheart! Come to Myrna, Becca. Oh, we're going to have such fun tonight." The little girl lunged out of Whit's arms toward an older woman with kinky steel-gray curls, and he reluctantly handed her over.

"Guess I know who's top dog around here. Hi, I'm Whit Montgomery." He extended his hand to the elderly woman.

"Pleased to meet you, Whit. I'm Myrna." She smiled slyly at him, then turned to Susannah. "If a man who looked like *that* picked *me* up, we'd have more than a business meeting!"

Susannah blushed scarlet as she extended a slip of paper. "Here's the number of the place I'll be."

Whit knew his own cheeks were slowly turning red, but he made a game effort to divert the woman's attention. "It was nice meeting you. Merry Christmas."

"Merry Christmas." Myrna held Becca out to Susannah. "Say bye-bye to Mommy, sweetie. Then we'll go play." Susannah clutched her daughter tightly before kissing the rosebud lips.

"'Bye, punkin. I love you. See you in the morning."

"Now, don't worry," Myrna said as she prepared to shut the door. "You know she'll be okay."

"I know." Susannah's voice was small. "Thanks again, Myrna."

"No trouble. Now you go on." Her eyes sparkled. "Don't want you to be late for your business." She cackled as she closed the door.

Whit picked up the bag Susannah had set on the floor. He placed the other hand under her elbow. "Shall we go?"

Susannah gave him a wan smile. "Yes. I'm sorry. I've never left her overnight before. I'm acting like a mother hen."

Whit thought her concern was perfectly normal. "You should've told me," he said. "We could've gotten a suite with two bedrooms and taken her along. Most large hotels have reputable baby-sitters who come in on request."

Susannah turned those huge violet eyes on him fully for the first time that evening. There was stunned amazement in their depths. "You'd have done that?"

He squirmed under her intent scrutiny, shrugging in feigned nonchalance. "If I'd realized you were going to worry, I'd have been glad to. She's a lovable child. I can understand why you don't like to leave her." He guided her down the hall to the front door. After helping her into the front seat of the car, he took a minute to place her bag into the trunk before coming around to the driver's seat.

Susannah was silent the whole way to the hotel. Whit glanced sideways at her every few minutes; she sat straight as a ruler, almost hugging the window. If he weren't so nervous himself, he would have laughed. But he was too worried about what he was going to say and do to get her to loosen up.

He retrieved their bags and escorted her up the steps, after tossing his keys to the young man waiting to park his car. Walking into the lobby, he told her, "I've already registered. Would you like to freshen up before dinner?"

"That would be fine."

Again, he wondered how he could draw her out of that shell of reserve. Maybe she'd unwind over drinks and dinner. But he wouldn't place a bet on it.

Their suite was on the seventh floor. Whit unlocked the door and motioned to Susannah to precede him.

"This is lovely." She walked to the door of the adjoining bedroom and glanced in, then turned and moved hastily back into the middle of the sitting room.

Trying to put her at ease, Whit searched for some innocent topic. "I haven't stayed in a hotel in quite some time. It'll be nice not to have to pick up my own towels." His words created an unexpected image in his head. He'd like to take a shower or a bath with this woman, to rub slick patterns over her smooth skin with soapy hands, to wash every inch of her creamy curves. Then he noticed she hadn't responded to his conversational gambit and another rush of nerves assailed him. How could they...get the job done...if she were this uptight?

Hastily he turned to the stereo over the television. Raucous music poured out when he switched it on and he grimaced. He fiddled with the tuner until he found a station pouring soft strains of mellow rock into the night. Then, looking around, he spotted the bar. "Would you like a drink?" He wasn't much of a drinker normally, but he needed to do something with his hands.

"No thanks, but you go ahead." She wandered over to the huge floor-to-ceiling window and opened the curtains. "Oh, what a view! I've always longed to live by the water."

He made himself a very dry martini. Carrying it carefully, he joined her at the window. The hotel was on the ocean. Although it was already dark outside, the moon was full and he could see the froth of the waves as they rushed in to lick and lap along the beach before sliding swiftly into the surf again.

"I love the ocean. I don't think I'd be happy if I got too far away from the sea." Whit cleared his throat. He hadn't meant to sound so impassioned.

Susannah twisted her head up and regarded him with a half smile. "It gets in your blood, doesn't it? I'll never live far away from it again, either," she confessed.

Whit pounced on the topic. "Where are you from?" She didn't have a Southern accent, but he couldn't figure out quite what she did have.

"I was born and raised in Ohio. I went to school in Athens, though. After I was married, we lived there for a time, but I moved down here to work for Ira after the divorce."

The divorce. He'd love to know more about her ex-husband, but he figured that was off-limits. "What did you study?"

"Early childhood education. I wanted to teach kindergarten."

"Do I hear a 'but' in there?"

She glanced at him again. "I dropped out and got married before I finished my student teaching."

He sensed it bothered her to admit it. "You could still finish your degree. My undergraduate degree is in biology. Then I did graduate work and my doctoral thesis on the turtles."

"The turtles?"

"Sorry. I forget that the whole world isn't into turtles. I study sea turtles."

"Aren't there several different kinds?"

"Very good." She'd surprised him. Many people knew less than nothing about sea turtles. "You're right. There are loggerheads, which I study. There are also hawksbills, greens, leatherbacks, olive ridleys, and *kemp's* ridleys."

"You must enjoy your work."

"I love it, but it can be frustrating because so many of them are vanishing."

"You mean becoming extinct?"

"Yeah. Being killed off is more like it." He didn't want to get fired up about the turtles tonight, though. In fact, he was having enough trouble not getting fired up just standing next to Susannah. He took a big slug of his drink.

Her hair curled softly around her shoulders. He was glad she hadn't put it up. It curled and bounced with every step she took. He touched a finger to one blond lock. "You have beautiful hair."

Skittishly, she stepped away, letting his finger hang in midair. "It's too curly. One drop of rain and I have cork-screw curls."

"It's pretty," Whit said firmly. He set down his drink as a sudden inspiration hit him. "Let's dance."

She looked positively astonished. "Dance?"

"Yeah. You know. Move our feet around the floor." He passed one arm around her waist and held her other in ball-room position. She felt fragile and light in his arms, as if one incautious move might snap delicate bones. "I'm not great, but I'm game. I'll try not to step on your feet."

She smiled. He liked the tiny dimple that came and went in her cheek when she relaxed. "I'm not great, either, but I enjoy it."

They moved slowly, gracefully around the furniture in the sitting room of the suite. They danced well together, he thought with satisfaction. She followed his limited leads nicely.

As they danced, Whit maneuvered her across the room until they were within feet of the bedroom door.

The bed. The reason they were here tonight. For the first time, he had sudden, shocking doubts about whether he could perform on command. This seemed so cold-blooded. Hell, it *was* cold-blooded! There was a snowball lodged in the pit of his stomach. Despite Susannah's warm body only inches away and the attraction he'd felt since they'd met, he didn't feel the slightest tingle of desire right now. What if he couldn't—

"You don't have to kiss me." Susannah refused to look him in the eye as she pulled away from him and stepped out of her shoes.

"Whoa, there." Preoccupied as he was with his own fears, the nerve he heard beneath her bravado gentled the hand he laid on her shoulder. He turned her around, a little surprised at how small she was in her bare feet. His own unease subsided beneath the need to reassure her when he saw how pale she was. "Why don't I have to kiss you?"

"Because. This is a business arrangement. I realize a man doesn't have to be wildly attracted to a woman to—what are you doing?"

Taking a deep breath, Whit slipped his arms around her waist. Deliberately, he pulled her close and nuzzled her neck. If she thought they were going to treat this like a business deal, she was sadly mistaken. He might be a little out of practice, but he'd never taken a woman in his life without the trappings of romance and he certainly wasn't going to start now. The thoughts whirling in his head were crowded out by more earthy concerns as he felt her trembling.

Her sweet, feminine fragrance was working its own melting magic on the ice in his gut and he began to wonder how he could get her to relax. "Actually, I've been worrying about whether or not I could please you," he confessed. "What makes you think I'm not attracted to you?"

Susannah was a marble statue, standing stiff and still in the low light. Her velvet dress had short, belled sleeves and he ran his palms clear up to her shoulders before retracing his path. A shiver chased over her, but still she didn't answer him.

"The day I saw you sitting outside Ira's office, I thought you were beautiful." Whit's voice was husky as he nibbled his way along her jaw. "My opinion hasn't changed." As his lips covered hers lightly, her long lashes swept down, veiling the glimmer of silver in her eyes. He drew her against him, holding her without making any further demands and slowly, her eyes opened. She didn't seem as rigid as she had a moment ago, but she was still tense.

His lips teased at hers, sliding back and forth over her soft, full mouth until slowly, tentatively, she began to kiss him back. Only then did he allow his tongue to sneak out and trace the seam of her lips. He licked, sucked and nibbled at her mouth, and finally, after long minutes, she allowed his tongue to part her lips and wander over the surface of her teeth. He'd expected to feel embarrassment at the necessity for this meeting. Instead, it felt more *right* than anything he'd done in a long time.

Encouraged by his success, Whit whispered, "Open your mouth for me."

Susannah whimpered far back in her throat.

The small sound inflamed him. The distinct stirring of male flesh beneath his trousers was a heady reassurance that he'd worried in vain. His hands traveled surely down over the smooth fabric of her dress, tracing the indentation of her spine until it deepened into a cleft between her buttocks. When he palmed the mounds of her bottom in his hands and pulled her snugly up against his aroused body she tensed again. He stopped his sensual assault, holding her intimately and continuing to kiss her, until she relaxed and her arms began to grip his biceps in rising need.

He was amazed at the strength of the desire that ripped through him. Susannah Taylor was a heady aphrodisiac, an unsuspected sensual feast for a man who'd prayed only for quiet enjoyment.

Her lips were soft, yet searing beneath his. She exuded a deep, dark feminine scent that wrapped around him and invaded every pore. It was totally at odds with her quiet porcelain appearance, so faint as to be unnoticed until a man was this close. When he pulled her against his body again, every cushioned curve, every dip and valley of female contour met him, caught him, melted against every male ridge and bulge, producing erotic reactions in his loins. Fire crackled, burning him alive.

He ran one hand down her bare back to where the fabric of the dress stopped his wandering hands. Unable to figure how to get her out of it, he slipped a hand over the sleek fabric covering her thighs until he reached the hem. Inching it up, he pulled her higher against him and inserted one leg between hers.

Susannah wrenched her mouth away. "Whit—"

Was he pushing her? Should he stop? The deep, secret flavor of the soft skin beneath her jaw lured him on and the thought was lost.

"Don't tell me to stop." He kissed a feverish path from her jaw to the neckline of her dress, licking along the obstruction. Fumbling with the fastenings at the back of the dress, he had it in a pool at her feet in seconds. Susannah gasped and attempted to cross her arms in front of her, but he caught her wrists and pulled them up to rest at his shoulders. Holding them there, he surveyed what the dress had covered.

Clad in a lacy demi-bra and tiny panties, a garter belt holding up her sheer stockings, her smooth flesh gleamed with the luster of a flawless pearl. She was every fantasy he'd ever had and a few he hadn't gotten around to yet. Releasing her wrists, his fingers followed the trail his tongue had taken, from one collarbone to the other. On the return journey, he dipped low to whisk over the tip of a breast.

Susannah cried out. Uncertainty assailed him again. Had he hurt her? "Do you like this?" He brought one hand down from her wrist to run a light circle around her nipple with his thumb. Just when he was prepared to concede defeat, she answered him.

"I . . . like it." Her voice was soft, hesitant, but the quick breath she sucked in when he rasped his nail across the beaded crest of her breast spoke volumes.

This couldn't be happening to him. She was more than he'd ever dreamed of, more than he'd ever longed for. "I want to touch you. Here." He kissed a taut pink nipple barely shielded by the bra. "Here." His mouth slid to her navel as he dropped to his knees. "Even here." He lightly pressed a kiss to the silky fabric covering her feminine secrets.

As Susannah's knees buckled, Whit caught her in strong arms, coming down onto the floor beside her before he gently removed her lingerie. Arousal warred with embarrassment as Susannah felt him step away. What was wrong with her? A near stranger was making her feel things she'd never known in three years of marriage. Making her want things she'd never imagined she could want, never knew she could need.

She lay trembling where he'd placed her, watching as he ripped off his clothes. Simple white cotton briefs barely contained the powerfully aroused masculinity she'd felt when he'd held her.

What would it be like when he was inside her? Her abdomen contracted involuntarily. She'd looked on this night as something to be endured, something to be gotten through and forgotten forever. In a flash of sudden clarity, she knew she'd never be able to forget this man as long as she lived.

She'd only had one lover before in her life. And she'd been stupid enough to marry him. Steve had been nothing like Whit Montgomery. Their sexual encounters had been quick and uninspiring, almost always carried out under cover of darkness. He'd never kissed her until she wanted to beg for more. He'd never run his hands over her skin as if she were a precious fur. And he'd certainly never been so... aroused... by her.

As Whit turned to take her in his arms, she realized even more fully how different he was from her ex-husband. Bigger, gentler, much more concerned about her reactions.... How odd that a stranger could make her feel more cared for, more exciting and more excited than the man to whom she'd been married.

He moved over her then, and she gave up the attempt at self-analysis. Perhaps she shouldn't enjoy this, but it might be the only time in her life she ever felt this way with a man. As his lips came down and a muscled thigh slid between her legs, she closed her eyes and gave herself up to sensation.

Whit groaned when she moved her thighs apart. She could feel him throbbing against her warm, wet flesh. His mouth trailed its way down her throat, claiming one nipple and suckling so strongly that she cried out and rocked restively beneath him. He slipped one hand down between their bodies and she gasped when he pressed boldly on her.

"Did I hurt you?" His voice was a rough growl.

"No...no..." She rolled her hips against his hand, telling him without words that he hadn't hurt her at all. Even as she spoke, one lean finger made a steady foray into the cleft it found. This time she cried out and he lifted his head from her breast to press fierce kisses into her mouth.

Whit let his weight come down on top of her and she gloried in the feel of her taut nipples rubbing against his furred chest. The finger that had been making such wonderful sensations in her abdomen suddenly slipped away, and she whimpered in protest.

"Shh," Whit commanded. "This is what you want." Using his legs to open her wider, he let her feel the hot strength of his aroused body. Susannah writhed against him, beyond any inhibition. Her body recognized its master in the hard, slick flesh probing at her feminine entrance and she arched her back, trying to embed him within her. Whit laughed softly. Then, as she dug her heels into the backs of his thighs, he surged forward in one mighty stroke, pressing himself deep inside her. The action released him from what control he'd held and with another strangled groan, he began to move, establishing a rhythmic push-and-pull that sent shocks of overwhelming sensation quivering up through her belly with every move he made.

Susannah was crying. To think that she could have lived all her life without experiencing this! As his rhythm deteriorated into a frantic maelstrom of movement, the force of her own approaching climax had her whimpering in small, repeated bursts of sound. When her body exploded and flowered beneath him, Whit shouted out his own completion, jerking spasmodically in surges that made her own body contract in response, spilling himself deep within her receptive well.

Whit shifted to one side, aware that he was probably crushing Susannah on the hard floor. He lifted his head

from its scented nest in the soft curve of her neck. His mind
wanted to shut down and simply savor the moment, but he
couldn't forget the instant of shock when he'd plunged into
her. She'd been so tight, so small, he'd have sworn she was
a virgin if it weren't for the daughter he'd seen with his own
eyes.

"Has it been a long time?"

"Yes."

"How long?"

"Since before Becca."

"Are you all right? I was—"

"Wonderful, but let's not analyze it."

He wondered whether she meant she felt wonderful or
he'd been. Silently he marveled at her incredible respon-
siveness. She made him feel more of a man than he'd ever
felt before.

Rolling to his feet in a single lithe move, he lifted her easily into his arms. She clutched at him a little frantically.

"I'm too heavy! Put me down."

"Compared to a three-hundred-pound turtle, you're a
feather." He peeled back the covers on the big bed and set
her gently in the middle of it.

Her voice held gentle humor. "Was that a compli-
ment?"

"Of course. I told you I spend a lot more time with them
than I do with people." He stretched out on his side,
throwing one leg over her smoother, smaller one. His hand
rested flat on her stomach, rotating in small circles. God, her
skin was fabulous. "Sorry about the floor. I guess I got
carried away."

"It's all right."

"Do you think one time will...do it?" He cursed himself silently as he felt the instant tension that invaded her
limbs.

Her voice was as stiff as the leg under his. "Statistically
speaking, probably. I read that sperm counts in subsequent
ejaculations within a given time period show—"

"Never mind." He exerted pressure until she sprawled on top of him, twining his fingers through her hair and pulling her mouth down on his.

They must've dozed. Susannah woke with a start. Memory flooded in, aided by the heavy weight of a hard male arm thrown over her waist. Whit had his head buried in her neck again, and his exhalations gusted against the sensitive flesh.

As her eyes adjusted to the dim light thrown by a single lamp, she saw that he'd kicked all the covers to the foot of the bed. She wondered if he routinely slept without covers.

His body was warm and heavy against her, inspiring a sweet sense of security. Resolutely she forced herself to acknowledge the memory of her uninhibited response to him. It wasn't in her nature to pretend the explosive passion between them had never happened. If she lived to be a hundred, she'd remember the feel of his hands on her body, the tantalizing tease of his tongue as it investigated female textures, the way his callused fingers had traced and tormented erotic places she hadn't known she had. If she lived to be a hundred, she'd never spend a day without thinking of the child they might have conceived tonight.

The last thought soured any pleasure in the simple act of lying close to him. Susannah lifted his arm and carefully began to slide from the bed. A quick shower and she could call a cab. It would be expensive, but she'd sooner scrape for a month than face him in the morning. She'd taken three steps toward the bathroom when a big hand captured her wrist and a single tug landed her back on the mattress. "Where are you going?"

Susannah blew the hair out of her eyes. "Home."

Whit raised one sable eyebrow. His hair stuck up at impossible angles and his jaw was shadowed by a major attack of stubble. He was adorable. More to convince herself than him, she repeated, "I want to go home now."

"In the middle of the night?" He stroked a finger over the curve of her shoulder. "I'll take you home in the morning."

She would not blush. She absolutely refused. But, as she felt his body hardening against her hip, it took a mighty effort of will to calmly repeat once more. "I want to go home now."

Three

___

Six weeks later Susannah pulled her battered compact car to a halt in the parking lot behind Ira's office. Her driver's window was down and vaguely the crash and roll of the ocean impinged upon her introspection. It was a typically warm winter day, the light breeze redolent with the scent of salt and sea.

She clutched the wheel tightly with both hands even though she'd turned off the engine. Deliberately, she took slow, deep breaths, concentrating on the rhythmic wash and wane of the waves to help her compose herself. Darn Whit Montgomery and his virility! Since their single night together, Susannah had been praying that she hadn't been fertile, that she hadn't conceived a child she'd have to give up—even to save Becca's life. It would've been an easy way out of the emotional upheaval conception would wreak on her.

But deep in her subconscious she'd known all along that she'd been as receptive to his seed as she'd been to his heated lovemaking that night. She couldn't afford to be this upset when she went into the office. Ira'd had doubts about her being a surrogate ever since she'd overheard him documenting the case into a tape recorder and talked him into letting her apply. If he saw her now, he'd scotch the whole deal.

If only she could afford to let him do exactly that!

Climbing out of her car, she headed into the building. Ira greeted her from the doorway of his office as she put her purse away in her desk drawer.

"Hi, Susannah. Was it yea or nay?"

She raised her head and looked him squarely in the eye. "I'm officially pregnant, Ira. You can notify Mr. Montgomery."

Ira's eyes raked over her intently. "Are you okay? You don't look so swift."

"I'm fine. I've been having more queasiness this time than I did with Becca. A couple of crackers should help. I missed my lunch." She shook her head. "Dumb."

"Well, I guess I'll try to get in touch with Turtle Island, then." Ira hesitated before he returned to his desk. "I could probably still get you out of this, Susannah. Are you sure?"

Susannah's heart leaped at his words, but she firmly squelched the hope. "I'm sure, Ira. I'm going to call Becca's doctor right now and set up her surgery." Her eyes brightened at the thought. "Oh, one more thing. When you talk to Wh—Mr. Montgomery, please tell him I'd prefer not to be remunerated until mid-March."

"Mid-March! But the terms of the contract specify that you can receive all but the final payment upon verification of positive pregnancy tests."

"I don't care. I'd prefer to wait until the first trimester ends. If anything goes wrong, it'll probably happen then."

"Did the doctor tell you anything I need to know?"

Susannah was startled. "Oh, no. It's just that since blood testing allows women to find out they've conceived in a matter of weeks now, people get their hopes up so early in a pregnancy. The statistical incidence of miscarriage hasn't changed much, despite modern medicine.''

Ira grimaced. ''I can hear myself explaining this to Whit.''

Four hours later Susannah removed her purse from the desk drawer and called a good-night to Ira. She still felt lousy. She'd been eating dry crackers like penny candy, but they hadn't done a thing for the nausea. She'd known for almost two weeks before she went to an obstetrician that she was pregnant. She'd had the same exact feeling of illness in the early days of her first pregnancy. But it hadn't been this severe.

Please let it go away soon. I can't deal with this on top of Becca's surgery and everything else. Everything else being preparing herself to hand the tiny life growing inside her to its father at birth and never seeing it again.

Determinedly she pushed aside that line of thinking and concentrated on Becca. Becca—who was going to be well in just a few short months! She'd made the appointment from work, and the surgery was scheduled for the first of March—just four weeks away. Her step quickened as she entered her building and picked up Becca from the sitter's. Entering her own small apartment, she sat down in the rocking chair with the still-sleeping child. The tiny, sweet-smelling body resting against her soothed the raw anguish she'd been carrying through the long day. Tenderly she examined her daughter's features, noting the gentle curve of the rosebud lips, the peaches and cream skin that was more cream than peaches these days, the dark lashes and brows that created a striking contrast to hair the same light shade as her mother's.

With concern, Susannah noted that her daughter's skin was pinched and bluish, her breathing shallow and irregular. She was eating like a bird. Could this surgery really wait for four more weeks?

Whit was on the dock in front of the boathouse with Axel, his handyman. Although it was only the middle of

February, the two men were in high gear as they began to prepare for the advent of the turtles onto the beaches in mid-May.

This week, they were overhauling the engines on the three motorboats, getting them ready for a summer of hard wear. Last week, they'd resealed all the canoes and checked the boats for structural damage. Whit had also inventoried the supplies of screen and pegs used to cover the turtle nests from animal predators, as well as all the other items the students would need.

Whit sang while he worked. He'd been singing even more than usual lately. He knew why, too. Ever since he'd gotten the message from Ira about Susannah Taylor's positive pregnancy test, he'd had butterflies in his stomach and nursery rhymes on his mind. Aware of Ira's warnings about the first trimester, Whit hadn't told Axel and his wife Hilda his news yet. God, he hoped they wouldn't think he was totally crazy!

Since he hadn't even known what a "first trimester" was when Ira'd called, he'd gone over to the mainland one day last week and bought every book he could find on prenatal concerns and fetal development. On his next trip, he'd figured he'd better pick up some child development information. After all, as a single parent, he was going to have to be doubly well-informed.

Axel had the doggone monitor on again. Whit enjoyed music while he worked. He could cheerfully go for weeks without speaking to anyone from the mainland. The nightly news gave him all the input he wanted from the outside world. Axel, on the other hand, was devoted to the mainland monitor that gave him all the dirt on his neighbors across the sound. It was a constant source of amusing aggravation to each of them, and they had a long-standing unofficial contest to see who could change the channel on the other more times during the course of a day.

"Glynn County Emergency Rescue Vehicle Number Four, please respond."

Whit sighed loudly enough to cover the technician's response to the dispatcher. "Haven't you had enough of this for one day, Axel? I'm getting mighty tired of singing to myself."

Axel snorted. "Do us both a favor, then, and quit it."

"...Child in respiratory distress. Transport to hospital requested."

"Give us the address again," requested the driver of the ambulance.

As the dispatcher repeated the address, Whit listened with half an ear—until he realized that the address being relayed was the same one he'd visited the night he'd taken Susannah out! In a state of panic, he leaped to his feet. Visions of the tiny blond girl he'd carried in his arms Christmas night flashed through his brain.

A screwdriver clattered to the deck and splashed into the water. He never heard it. A powerful voice inside his head was urging him to go to Susannah. His fists clenched at his sides as he fought the impulse.

It wouldn't be wise to get too friendly with her.

But this is different. She might need support.

Her voice rang in his ears. *This is going to be difficult as it is.*

Right. I'd be crazy to involve myself in her problems.

But she might need me.

"Axel, get the cruiser. I've got to get to the mainland!"

Whit grabbed a bicycle from the rack. He raced up the crushed shell path to the big house, cursing all the way because he hadn't brought a Jeep down today. He slammed in the front door and took the stairs two at a time.

"Hilda, I need an overnight bag!" He shucked off his filthy clothes and raced into the bathroom.

Hilda came puffing up the stairs, grumbling about the mess he'd left on the floor. "What's the meaning of this, young man?"

Whit grinned, despite his hurry. He'd be a young man to the housekeeper when he was fifty and she was eighty. "I have to get to the mainland and I don't know when I'll be back. The child of a friend of mine is ill. Can you pack me a bag?''

Hilda could move with surprising speed when the occasion demanded it. By the time he'd washed and changed into clean clothes, she was handing him his bag and his keys and hustling him out the door. Axel had done better than just getting the boat; he'd gotten a Jeep to drive Whit back down to the dock.

Gratefully, Whit jumped in, remembering too late why he never rode anywhere with Axel. The vehicle shot down the path like an angry hornet as Whit clung to his bag with one hand and the seat with the other. Soon they were at the dock. Barely pausing, he stowed his gear and cast off, waving thanks to Axel.

''I'll call you on the monitor,'' he shouted over the roar of the engine.

Axel nodded, waving to show he'd heard.

It wasn't until Whit had docked the boat and unlocked the garage where he kept the Mercedes that he had time to think about what he was doing. His move had been impulsive, totally at odds with his usual methodical plod.

But when he'd heard that Becca was having trouble breathing, he'd known he needed to be there. Susannah might need him. She hadn't appeared to have much other support in her life.

In rising panic, he wondered what had happened to Becca. Maybe she'd swallowed something. Little kids loved to taste things, didn't they? He prayed she'd still be alive when he got to the hospital. He screeched to a halt in a no-parking zone and raced into the emergency entrance.

Susannah was standing by the single window at the far end of the long, angled room to which he was directed. One hand was wrapped protectively around her own waist, the other crushed a tissue to her lips.

''Susannah?''

Although his voice was as soft as he could make it, he winced at the rough sound of his fear echoing in the silence. Susannah jumped and turned. Her eyes were red and swollen, and her mouth quivered as she said his name.

"Whit!"

She met him in the middle of the room. Holding out her hand as if to shake his, she tried to speak, but her breath caught on a sob. Distance be damned. Taking her hand, he pulled her against him.

That was all it took. Wrapping her arms around his neck, Susannah buried her face in his shoulder. Her tears were soaking his shirt but he didn't notice. He cuddled her close as sobs shook her slender frame. Even through his fear for Becca, the sweet feel of her curves aligning perfectly with his registered. Impatient with himself, he shoved the thought aside.

"What happened to Becca? Calm down. Talk to me." He spoke in a low, soothing voice, only half aware of the words he repeated, concentrating all his attention on the woman he held.

The tempo of Susannah's sobbing gradually slowed until at last she gave a mighty sigh. The warmth of her breath gusted against his neck and her body relaxed in his grasp. Pulling back slightly, she reached behind her and unlocked his hands at her waist.

"Let's sit down and I'll tell you about Becca." She led him over to an orange vinyl sofa.

Whit sank down beside her. Their knees brushed as she angled herself to face him. He took her hands in a reassuring grip. "I heard an ambulance called for Becca on the mainland monitor. What happened?"

Susannah hitched in a deep breath. "Becca has a congenital heart defect. She was scheduled for surgery next month to correct it, but I knew she wasn't doing well. This morning, she couldn't get her breath. Myrna couldn't help her, so she called for assistance. When the doctor saw her, he decided to operate now instead of waiting. He said—"

Her voice broke, but she leveled it and went on. "He said she wouldn't live another month if he didn't fix the problem now."

Whit was stunned. This was totally beyond the scope of all his imaginings. Images came back to haunt him. The little girl hadn't walked at all the night he'd seen her. She'd been sweet, but unusually quiet compared to the wild toddlers he'd seen in stores. And he remembered that porcelain complexion.

Fear congealed in his gut. A congenital defect! He wanted to ask why he'd seen no mention of it in Susannah's medical history. Suddenly, mixed in with his concern for Becca was a gripping anxiety. Could the baby Susannah was carrying now develop such a problem? He desperately wanted to ask, but when he looked at Susannah's pale, strained features, he couldn't bring himself to introduce the troubling topic.

"Is Becca in surgery now?"

Susannah nodded. "They'll let me know as soon as she's finished." Her eyes told him the doctor's words could shatter her world.

Whit slid back against the sofa's uncomfortable cushions. "Then I'll wait with you." He pulled her into the curve of his arm.

With a heartfelt exhalation of exhaustion, Susannah laid her head against his shoulder. "You're a good man."

Two hours passed. Neither of them spoke much. Susannah was by nature a reserved person; she suspected Whit was the same.

What should she say to him? She'd been stunned when he came striding into the waiting room. She'd wanted to throw herself into his arms. But she knew she couldn't let him get too close.

That thought had lasted until his arms had gone around her.

But now, sitting in the curve of his arm on the uncomfortable cushion, she couldn't think of a single thing to say.

Although she felt more comfortable and cared for leaning against him than she'd ever felt with Steve, she knew this couldn't continue. In seven months, Whit would take her— no, *his*—baby and vanish from her life. She had to be ready.

In addition to all her black thoughts, she was still plagued by nausea. It was worse than usual today because she'd left the office so fast she hadn't even grabbed her sweater, much less any of the crackers she kept in a desk drawer all the time.

Now Susannah's stomach was rebelling. Lying against Whit, her fear for Becca was oddly diminished. His solid presence made her feel safer and more protected than she could ever remember feeling before.

If only she didn't throw up. She took long, slow breaths, trying to stave off the waves of sickness rolling over her.

"You doing okay?" Whit's voice was a low growl in her ear.

She couldn't even turn her head to look at him for fear the motion would upset her precarious control of her stomach. "Yes. Just a little . . . morning sickness."

She caught Whit's glance at his functional waterproof watch out of the corner of her eye. "It's two o'clock in the afternoon. I thought morning sickness went away after you ate a few crackers for breakfast."

Just the mention of food made Susannah's stomach heave in warning. She sucked in a quick breath and willed her rising gorge to back down. "My stomach can't tell time. This is worse than the last pregnancy. It lasts all day long."

"What can I do to help?"

She risked turning her eyes in his direction. "Would you mind going down to the cafeteria and getting me a couple of packs of dry crackers, please? I have to try to get something down. And a glass of water might help."

Whit gently slid his arm out from under her head without jostling her. "I'll be right back. Hang tight."

He was back faster than she would've believed possible. He unwrapped the crackers and offered her one, watching with worried eyes as she took a small experimental bite.

"Somehow I never imagined the discomfort a woman has to endure during pregnancy."

Thank God. The cracker was staying down. Greedily she devoured two more and drank several sips of water before smiling dryly at him. "You think this is bad? You should try walking with a fifteen-pound load in your tummy. Or worse, those last days after the baby drops and you feel like you have a basketball between your legs. The baby presses on your bladder, you can't sleep in one position for more than ten minutes, and you walk like you just got off a very wide horse. And then there's labor—"

"I get the idea. It's a good thing men don't have to do this. The human race would become extinct."

"It's not a lot of fun," Susannah admitted. "But it's all worth it in the end. It's amazing how fast you forget all the discomfort when you begin to cuddle that little bundle." She fell silent, recalling that she wouldn't have that particular joy this time. Pain contracted her heart into a tight fist.

Whit was still kneeling in front of her. His eyes dropped and she knew he was thinking the same thing. As he opened his mouth to say something, a doctor appeared in the doorway.

Susannah scrambled to her feet. The room swayed alarmingly, and she felt Whit grab her around the waist. "Careful."

"Good news, Mrs. Taylor." This doctor didn't beat around the bush. "Rebecca's in recovery. She weathered the surgery very well, given the condition of the atrophied tissue we found. I replaced it as we discussed earlier and repaired the surrounding muscle. With any luck at all, Rebecca will be walking in a few days. As the heart begins to function more efficiently, we should see a return to a more normal activity level." The doctor smiled. "I have a two-year-old grandson. No question about it, you're going to be a busy lady."

Susannah closed her eyes for a long minute. "Thank you," she whispered.

The doctor patted her shoulder. "A nurse will come get you when they're ready for you in the recovery room. I'll look in on her in the morning. Write down all your questions and you can ask them then. Most people find they think of a million things *after* the doctor leaves."

Susannah nodded.

Whit extended his hand. "Thanks again, Doctor. She's a special little ray of sunshine."

The waiting room was silent after the doctor's departure. Susannah stood in the middle of the room with Whit at her side. Hot tears slid down her cheeks. She hadn't cried so much since she'd learned of Becca's life-threatening heart defect.

The relief was overwhelming. For two years she'd lived with the knowledge that Becca was critically ill. For two years she'd watched as Becca's energy gradually dwindled to a trickle.

"I'm sorry," she managed as Whit wiped at her tears and directed her toward a chair.

"You should be. This is happy news. I don't know what to do with women who cry. Help me out, okay?"

She smiled at his exasperation. "Okay." How could she explain the feelings with which she was dealing? "I've always lived with the fear of losing her. It's hard to switch gears. I feel a hundred pounds lighter."

Whit returned her smile. "I'm pretty relieved myself. But why in the world did you wait until it became an emergency situation to correct it?"

Susannah sighed. He hadn't sounded critical, only curious. "When Becca was diagnosed, she was too small to have survived the surgery. They told me if I could put it off for a year or so, she'd stand a much better chance of coming through it. After my husband left, finances were tight and I wanted to save as much as I could before she had the operation. Until recently, she was holding her own, but the past two months or so have been scary." She shook her head. "I still can't believe it's over. She's going to be fine in a few months!"

There was a small silence. She came out of her euphoria long enough to notice that Whit didn't share her delight. His craggy features bore a look of... concern, almost, and his dark blue eyes looked worried.

"What's the matter?" She squeezed his arm, feeling the solid muscles beneath her fingertips.

"Can I ask you something?" He barely gave her time to nod before he plunged into his question. "If it was congenital, why isn't Becca's heart problem mentioned in your medical history?"

She understood immediately. Remorse hit her with the force of a strong breaker in the surf. "This baby will be fine," she said, placing a protective hand over her abdomen. "Becca's heart trouble is a congenital malformation—but it runs in her father's family. In fact, I'm lucky she's alive. Most of the Taylor children born with it don't survive." She knew her tone carried traces of bitterness and she strove to erase them from her voice. Whit was already looking at her strangely.

"But you chose to take the risk of bearing a child, knowing it might inherit the defect?"

Her answer was as expressionless as his query. "I didn't know about it when Becca was conceived." She could see more questions filling his eyes as steadily as a faucet would fill a pitcher, but a bustling in the hallway preceded a white-uniformed nurse into the waiting room.

"Would you like to see your daughter now, Mrs. Taylor?"

Susannah jumped to her feet, looking over her shoulder at Whit even as she started forward. "I don't know how long I'll be. You don't have to stay if you don't want to."

Her words left an unspoken plea in the air between them.

Whit motioned her on. "I'll meet you in her room in a little while. Give her a big kiss for me."

Her nose woke up first. What in the world was that smell? Then the rest of her body began to make itself known. She was about as uncomfortable as she thought she could possibly get.

Her feet were freezing. One arm was completely numb. Her neck ached from being bent at some weird angle, and her eyes felt as if they were wired shut. She was *still* nauseous.

But what was that odor?

Cautiously, Susannah opened one eye a slit. It was dark in the room, but the outline of the crib seared into her mind and memory rushed back. Becca. Operation. Whit. She could hear Becca's breath wheezing in and out. The sound was blessedly reassuring. Turning her head a bit, she was confronted with a pair of large, sock-clad feet propped on the arm of her chair less than a foot from her nose.

Feet. Whit's feet. Socks. Yup, that's what the smell was. She smiled to herself. He'd be mortified when he woke up. Did she dare tease him? He was so serious.

And so sweet. He wouldn't have had to rush in to the hospital when he'd heard the news. His concern for her daughter had been real. His concern for her had been a surprise. One to which she could easily become addicted. Wistfully she admitted to herself how nice it would be to share all the little joys and worries of parenting with someone like Whit Montgomery. He exuded gentleness and caring concern. He was as different from her self-absorbed, self-indulgent ex-husband as the warm sun was from the cool distance of the moon.

Oh, well. She was about as likely to interest Whit as she was to go to the moon, too. They'd engaged in a business arrangement. He was just making sure she took care of herself.

Reaching out with the arm that had feeling, she trailed a finger from the heel of one large foot up over the ball and back down. Whit mumbled and shifted in the chair he'd pulled up at an angle to hers. Susannah repeated the motion on the sole of the other foot. This time, the feet plunked to the floor and Whit sat up in his chair with a loud groan. "What time is it?"

Susannah turned her head further. "Good question. I don't know the answer."

"Why were you torturing my feet? I was in the middle of a wonderful dream."

That piqued her interest. "Featuring a well-built woman, no doubt." Now where had that come from? Thank God it was dark!

She caught the flash of Whit's grin. "No, actually it was about turtles. I'd just convinced a whole roomful of shrimpers to use TEDs on their nets." He snorted. "I should be so lucky."

Susannah wondered if he were speaking the same language she was. "You lost me. What are TEDs? And shrimpers?"

"A TED is a Turtle Exclusion Device. It's a sort of basket that diverts turtles who swim into the shrimp fishermen's—shrimpers'—nets. Shrimpers are notorious for their turtle mortality statistics. They keep their nets out so long, any trapped turtles drown before the nets are hauled up. Part of my efforts to save the turtles from extinction is to educate fishermen about the value of TEDs. The devices became mandatory a few years ago, but a lot of shrimpers still aren't using them regularly."

His voice took on shades of bitterness. "Unfortunately many of them are too concerned with making a buck to worry about the extinction of a few species of 'worthless turtles.'"

"That's terrible. What else do you do to save the turtles?"

Whit hesitated, and for a minute she thought he wasn't going to answer her. Then he spoke quietly. "My family's estate encompasses Turtle Island. The island is a nesting ground for huge numbers of loggerheads every spring and summer. Turtles are sort of like salmon—they return every other year or so to the same spot to lay their eggs. Unlike salmon, they don't die after laying their eggs. I offer a six-week course for college students four times throughout the summer. I teach the students about all aspects of turtle conservation and management while they're monitoring the nests and recording numbers of returning turtles and hatchlings."

Susannah was fascinated. "How did you get interested in that?"

"I grew up on the island. I've been turtle-watching since I was a kid. Some of the turtles that come in each year are old friends I've been seeing for nearly twenty years."

Becca stirred in her sleep and Susannah's attention was immediately diverted. Wincing a little as her body protested the movement, she rose and went to her daughter's side. Becca looked so defenseless in the hospital crib, attached to all sorts of lines and monitors. Susannah pressed her knuckles against her eyes to stem the ready tears that rose.

She jumped as Whit came up beside her. She hadn't heard him rise from the chair.

"How's she doing?"

Susannah warmed to the genuine worry coloring his tones. "All right, I think. The nurse should be in again soon to check her." She gestured through the glass window that allowed the nurses to keep a close eye on patients in critical care.

"How are *you* doing?"

He must've noticed the evidence of her crying. "I'm okay. It just hits me every once in a while that she's going to be fine. It's hard to absorb. On the other hand, it breaks my heart to see her like this and know how much pain she's enduring." Her voice broke. "It just isn't fair. Toddlers are supposed to be running headlong and exploring, shouting and giggling all day, not lying in hospital beds with a huge row of stitches in their chests." Fiercely she dashed away the tears. "When you first hold that precious little body in your arms, you want to protect her and give her everything she ever wants. You assume good health is guaranteed. It's hard to admit you aren't capable of keeping the hurt away forever, but it's worse when she's this small. Becca thinks Mommy can make anything right in her world and I feel so helpless—"

"Shh." Whit gathered her against his broad chest, passing one arm behind her back and using the other hand to wipe her cheeks. "You can't change this now. There's no point in tearing yourself to pieces over it. Look forward. Never look back. Becca will soon be on the mend. It's fortunate she is so young. This memory will fade pretty fast."

Heaven. Resting against Whit, feeling the solid strength of his arms around her and one callused thumb rubbing over her cheek, all Susannah could think of was that this was a small slice of heaven. Had she ever felt so cherished? At the same instant she became aware of the hard length of his body flush against hers, the intimate thrust of his thighs at the soft flesh of her belly. Her mind was flooded with memories she'd buried under the weight of concern for Becca. She'd also avoided thinking about Whit because ever since they'd consummated the contract, she'd felt guilt that she so enjoyed his lovemaking that night.

Hastily, she pulled away from him. "You're right. I need to think positively." Seeking to restore the atmosphere of casual friendship between them, she tried for a wry tone. "Sorry. My hormones are in an uproar right now. I'm not normally so weepy."

Whit's face was impassive as a nurse bustled in to take Becca's vitals. His voice was brusque. "I'm going to take a walk. Why don't you stretch out in both chairs for a while?"

Four

___

Whit was growing more and more concerned about Susannah.

This morning she'd turned positively green when he'd mentioned breakfast and she'd flatly refused to leave Becca's side to get any lunch. When he'd offered to bring some up, she'd declined, saying she only wanted a few more packs of crackers.

Was it possible for a woman to get so sick she miscarried? He didn't know much about pregnant women, but the thought scared him stiff. After the third time she'd bolted for the bathroom during the afternoon, he decided enough was enough.

When she came slowly out of the small room, he was waiting by the door. Taking her elbow, he led her back to her seat.

"Do you feel this bad all the time?"

Susannah looked startled. "Oh, no. At least, I didn't when I was carrying Becca. I do feel worse this time, but if

I can get through a few more weeks, I'll begin to feel better. Morning sickness usually abates after the first trimester.''

"So how much longer will that be?"

"Three or four weeks."

"This concerns me, Susannah. You seem pretty sick. Do you think there's any danger of losing the baby?"

Susannah's violet eyes darkened. "The baby will be fine, Whit. I wouldn't take any chances with your child."

Whit was running out of patience. "I don't care about the child! I mean, I do, but—" He gave her an exasperated glare. "I was thinking about *you*."

Susannah held her rigid posture a moment longer. Then he could see the tension ease from her stance. "I'm sorry. Thank you for your concern, but I really don't believe it's a serious problem."

And that was that. Case dismissed. Whit could read it in her final tone. Well, if she were certain it wasn't a serious problem.... He sought for a safe topic that would keep them out of any turbulent waters. And keep his mind off her body. He'd swear that already her breasts were fuller; they strained against the fabric of her blouse as if they'd spill out momentarily.

Becca moaned and Susannah rushed to her bedside. Whit was right behind her. The tot was waking more frequently today and she was becoming much more alert as the afternoon wore on.

"Hi, baby. How's my girl feeling?" Susannah smoothed fair hair away from the little girl's forehead tenderly.

"Wan' dink, Mom-mee."

Susannah obliged, holding a cup with a straw down for the child. Becca apparently didn't know how to use a straw yet, because Susannah used her finger over one end to draw liquid into the straw and transfer it to Becca's mouth. Whit watched her repeat the tedious task again and again. His apprehension grew as he realized that when Susannah handed his child over to him, *he'd* be responsible for all these little parenting tricks. *He'd* be the one who was as powerful as God in the eyes of his child. An understanding of what Susannah had meant last night raced through him, and he found that he was actually shaking.

Was he crazy to consider this? He didn't know anything about babies.

Another unpleasant thought struck him. Babies were born all the time with life-threatening problems and they weren't always inherited as Becca's had been. Could his baby be born with something similar? Not if he could help it, he thought with a surge of protectiveness. Susannah was going to have the best of care throughout this pregnancy. To get his mind off his worries, he leaned over the crib. "Hi, Becca. Do you remember me?"

Violet eyes widened, but the child only studied him. He offered her a finger, which she clasped without hesitation in a surprisingly strong grip.

Susannah encouraged her. "Remember Mommy's friend, Becca?"

Whit caught the gleam in Becca's eye an instant before she croaked, "Whit!"

Whit grinned. "Very good."

Susannah shook her head. "I can't believe she remembered your name. She hasn't seen you in two months."

"I made a good impression. Go over there and look in the bags in the closet." Whit turned back to the child still holding his finger. "Becca, Mommy has something for you. You were a good girl yesterday. Would you like a present?"

A grin crinkled the tot's eyes. "P'esent for Bec-ca?"

"You bet," Whit promised her. "Just a minute." He turned to where Susannah was pulling three bags from the closet. Her face was a study in amazement.

"Just where did you go yesterday?" she demanded.

Whit grinned self-consciously. "I got a few things to keep Becca busy while she's recuperating. You can give them to her."

Susannah's eyes filled with tears. "You're incredible. You give them to her."

"No." Whit's tone was unshakable. "Her mommy should give her the first one." He pulled out a cuddly white harp seal puppet. "I thought this was pretty cute. Think she'll like it?"

Susannah's eyes brimmed again but she made an effort to smile. "Are you kidding? It's adorable." Picking up the seal, she returned to the bed.

Whit thumbed through the book he'd bought. It was about a little monkey who had an operation. He hoped Becca would enjoy it.

He could hear Becca's delighted squeals as he approached the crib. Susannah was on her knees beside the crib, making the seal "talk" to Becca.

"Me's, Mom-mee, me's!" Becca was demanding.

Laughing, Susannah rose and handed the puppet to her daughter. "It's a baby seal, Becca. Can you say 'seal'?"

Becca already had the puppet on the tiny arm that wasn't hooked up to an IV. It reached nearly to her shoulder. "Se-ah, Whit? Se-ah?"

"I see your seal," he answered gravely. "What's his name?"

Becca gave him a long, considering stare. He was about to suggest something harmless like "Sammy" when she burst out, "Whit!"

"Oh, I think there are—" he began.

"Whit is a lovely name for your seal, Becca." Susannah cut him off neatly. "Would you like to take a nap with Whit now?"

The little girl's eyelids were drooping but she shook her head.

"I'll sing to you," Susannah cajoled.

Becca shook her head again. "Whit sing." She turned her head to face him. "Whit sing. P'ease?"

Whit laughed. "How can I resist that?"

Susannah smiled. "She likes nursery rhymes."

"Nursery rhymes, huh?" Whit smiled at the child clutching the soft white seal that was half as big as she was.

"I can manage a few of those. Will you close your eyes while I sing?"

Smiling triumphantly, the sleepy child nodded.

Susannah sat quietly in the vinyl chair. The man was amazing. He had told her that he'd never spent much time around children. She found it hard to credit. He displayed an instinctive rapport with Becca. Susannah wondered if he had any idea how awkward many bachelors felt around small children.

Well, she couldn't fault him. He was going to be a good father. The toys he'd selected for Becca were thoughtful and appropriate. She'd questioned him about a turtle puppet and several other items she'd noticed in the bags, and he'd sheepishly admitted they were for the baby. His words had sent a pang straight to her heart, but another part of her rejoiced that he was so involved with his impending parenthood already.

Becca's eyes were glued to Whit's face, though she fought a losing battle with the sandman. By the time the last notes of the tune had drifted into silence, the little girl was fast asleep, still clutching her seal. When Whit moved from the side of the crib, Susannah slid her feet off his chair and beckoned him to come sit down.

"You sing beautifully." Her voice rang with sincerity.

"Thanks." Whit flushed, clearly uncomfortable.

"Have you ever taken lessons?"

"You mean, voice?" At her nod, Whit grimaced. "Hardly. I grew up on an isolated island, remember? Until I was ready for high school, my grandfather was my teacher."

Susannah was shocked. "You mean nobody else lives there?" When Whit shook his head, she rushed on. "I pictured a small village. I didn't realize you meant *nobody* was around."

"It wasn't so bad. I loved the island, and I was too busy with the wildlife to feel I was missing anything." She could see him make a conscious effort to lighten his defensive tone. "It never hit me how isolated our lives were until I got to be around fourteen and started thinking about girls. And my own circumstances changed then, anyway."

"What happened?"

"I was sent to a boarding school on the mainland. It was close by, so I still got to come home every weekend."

Susannah stared at him in horrified fascination. "I can't imagine being so isolated. What if you get sick? Or hurt?"

"We're in touch with the mainland by monitor. A helicopter flies in for emergencies."

"There's no other way to get there?" She was feeling more and more astounded by the minute.

"Boat," he answered tersely. "We go for supplies and mail once a week. Those of us who live on Turtle Island aren't all that keen on the social whirl, so it's not exactly a hardship."

"You like the isolation." Susannah stated the fact as if she couldn't quite comprehend such an occurrence.

"Love it."

"How did you feel when you went away to school?" It wasn't hard to visualize a backward teenage boy leaving home for the first time. She could feel her heart reaching out to that boy.

"It wasn't as bad as I'd first feared. I made friendships that helped ease the initial loneliness."

"And then you went away to college?"

"Yeah. I enjoyed it, but my heart always wanted to get back to the island."

"Whit..." Susannah hesitated. "I know this is none of my business, but I'm curious. Do you plan to raise our— *your*—child on the island like you were raised?"

Whit lifted an eyebrow, but he didn't take offense. "I hope to," he replied evenly. "I'm not sure about the details, but I can't imagine leaving. I want my child to grow up with a love for his or her heritage."

"But isn't it dangerous?" she blurted.

Whit's head came up. "In what way? Sure, there are a few natural hazards, but there are no automobile accidents, no violent crimes, no worries about your child getting snatched on the way home from school...." He shrugged. "It's all relative, Susannah. You're familiar with the hazards of mainland life. I'm confident that life on the island is far less dangerous overall."

He sounded as if he pitied her shortsighted view, and his critical tone stung.

"I can't imagine living out in the sticks like that. It's no wonder you like those turtles better than people."

"Those turtles are one heck of a lot less trouble than most of the people I know." His voice was tight and angry.

Hearing the sharp retort, Susannah was immediately contrite. True, Whit's life-style would never suit her. It sounded far too restrictive. But who was she to judge others? Whit had been kinder to her than she'd ever expected. Clearly he hadn't grown up missing anything vital in his emotional makeup.

Heaving a sigh, she offered a quiet apology. "I'm sorry. I have no right to criticize your way of life simply because I find it hard to understand."

"I'm glad you recognize that." He was still angry.

"You've been wonderfully helpful to me, and I appreciate your assistance." She risked a small joke. "Especially since I'm not a turtle."

Whit was silent for a long minute. Just when she'd opened her mouth to add more embellishment to her thanks, he responded. "It's true I don't often think of other people. In that respect, maybe my upbringing was a little lax."

"I bet you couldn't resist that turtle puppet," she teased, wanting to lighten the serious tone of their discussion.

Whit studied his toes, stretched out before him in front of the chair, but he accepted her change of topic. "I got to thinking I'd better start preparing the physical setting."

His quaint choice of words made Susannah laugh. "Yes, there are a few details you'll need for the 'physical setting.'"

"Like what?" He raised his head. She could almost see him preparing to make a mental list.

"You'll have to have a crib for the first two years, more or less. And a changing table. Diaper pails. Lots and lots of diapers. Newborns need to be changed roughly sixteen times a day, whether you use disposables or cloth."

"Holy cow!" He looked stunned. "How long does *that* last?"

Susannah smiled. "Oh, about as long as it takes you to get good and sick of doing it. By six months, you're down to six or eight changes a day, I'd say."

"I'll need to learn how to wash diapers. Or at least," he amended, "I'll need to be able to teach Hilda how to do it."

"Who's Hilda?" Susannah couldn't help it. The question was out before she could stop it. She had envisioned him living a solitary life on his island, but for all she knew, he could have a live-in lover. She straightened in her chair. "I'm sorry, that was rude. Just tell me to mind my own business."

Whit waved one lean hand. "No problem. Hilda is my housekeeper. She practically raised me. She and Axel—her husband—have no children. They've been on the island since my grandfather hired them right after they were married."

A ridiculous wave of...relief?...rolled through Susannah. *Get a grip, girl,* she scolded herself. *When Whit leaves here, you'll never see him again. He'll go back to his island alone. It's better that way. You can't get attached to this baby. If you're involved with its father, you're asking for trouble.*

Whit interrupted her sober thoughts. "Has the doctor said anything about when you could expect to take Becca home?"

"I asked him this morning," Susannah confessed. "He didn't want to commit himself, but he said she was looking pretty good, and if she gets along as well as he expects, maybe she'll be discharged Thursday or Friday."

Whit whistled in surprise. "That's fast."

Susannah nodded. "They keep open-heart patients less than a week now, and children naturally heal quickly. Ira's been very understanding, but I'm hoping to get back to work in two weeks or so."

"Ira's a good guy," Whit said. "Let me know when she's discharged. I'll come over and take you home."

Susannah was shocked. "No. I appreciate the offer, but you've done so much already. I don't want to take you away from your work."

"I'll come over when you're ready to take her home." Whit's tones were measured, unyielding. "You can't carry her up three flights of stairs, not to mention all the stuff you're going to have, as well. It's not a crime to let me help you, Susannah."

She was silent, unwilling to accept his assistance. No, it wasn't a crime. But it could be heartbreak if she couldn't keep herself emotionally distanced from this compelling man.

Distance. That was the only way to handle him.

Whit stood on the sidewalk beside Susannah's apartment, on the Friday that Becca was discharged, experiencing a curious sense of déjà vu. He remembered the last time they'd stood here. It reminded him of the night they'd shared, and erotic memories stirred in his loins.

Susannah had treated him like a very comfortable, very casual old friend all week. Her courteous manner hadn't slipped once since the day they'd nearly argued over his living location. In no way did she hint that she remembered the sexual fire that had burned between them with the same vivid recollection he did.

"Well," Susannah took a deep breath as Myrna carried Becca into the building. "Thank you for everything."

"You're very welcome. Glad I could be of help." Whit felt ridiculous when she held out her hand, but he took it anyway, holding it lightly in his own rough palm. "Let me know if you need anything."

Susannah gave him a valiant smile. "We'll be fine. Ira will always know how Becca's getting along. I'm sure he'll keep you informed."

In other words, she didn't want to hear from him again. That was a given, under the circumstances. It wasn't wise. He didn't want to get involved with her, either.

Slowly he released her hand. Her soft flesh slipped through his fingers like the finest silk as she turned away.

Five weeks later a light knock on the door preceded Myrna and Becca as they came trooping into Susannah's apartment from a jaunt down to the playground. Becca was bouncing up and down, chattering at the baby-sitter, and Susannah took a moment to savor the incredible recovery her daughter had made from her surgery. She'd hardly believed the doctor when he warned her how great children's recuperative powers were.

She gulped in a deep breath as she sat up on the sofa, leaning her head back and trying to calm her roiling stomach. She'd been off work for the past two weeks battling nausea.

"Myrna me's horsie!" Becca announced as she slid from the older woman's back.

"I see." Susannah fought to keep her voice light.

"Mom-mee Bec-ca horsie, too?"

Susannah bit her lip as she shook her head. "I'm sorry punkin. Mommy can't play horsie today. Are you ready for dinner?"

"No dinner. *Horsie.*" There appeared to be a direct correlation between Becca's good health and the degree of defiance she exhibited. As far as Susannah was concerned, the Terrible Twos couldn't have come at a worse time.

"Are you still dragging around with this flu?" Myrna looked over Becca's flaxen head, assessing Susannah's face as Becca persisted in a repetitive singsong monotone with her request.

Susannah hesitated. She'd been wondering how to break her news to Myrna. When Becca lost interest in a horsie ride and went bouncing into her bedroom, Susannah knew there would be no better opportunity.

"It isn't the flu," she said quietly.

Myrna's head jerked up. "What, then?" There was fear in her voice, and Susannah realized she was envisioning a fatal disease.

"I'm not sick," she said hastily. "I'm pregnant."

Myrna just looked at her. Susannah couldn't read her expression. "You're pregnant?" she repeated at last.

"Yes."

"Are you getting married, then?"

Susannah closed her eyes briefly. This was the tough part. She'd already realized that after the baby was born, she and Becca would have to move away. She couldn't take the chance of Becca ever learning about this—situation—as she grew older. "No, I'm not getting married."

Myrna was silent again. Then she blurted, "Is it that fella you were with on Christmas?"

Susannah felt her face growing red. "I'd prefer not to discuss the baby's father," she said gently, hoping she could get through this without damaging the friendship she'd enjoyed with the older woman.

Myrna snorted. "All right. I know it's none of my business. But people around here don't hold with this kind of foolin' around. Your boss isn't goin' to be too happy when he finds out you're knocked up. What if you lose your job?"

"I've already told my employer." Susannah didn't think Ira would mind if she stretched the truth a bit. "He's been very kind. He's hired a temporary until this sickness passes."

"You close to four months yet?" Although Myrna's face was still set in disapproving lines, she was thinking of the practicalities to be considered. Susannah nodded, grateful that Myrna hadn't reacted in horror, but she knew she daren't tell the grandmotherly woman the true story. Myrna never would condone Susannah's decision to become a surrogate for Whit Montgomery.

"Mom-mee be horsie." Becca wandered into the room again. She still hadn't given up on her theme song.

"No, Becca. Mommy's going to make you some dinner." The very thought sent Susannah's stomach into a gymnastic routine.

"Why don't I feed Becca and take her over to my apartment to play? Then you can rest a little longer."

Too nauseated to do more than agree, Susannah gratefully murmured "Thank you, Myrna" before shuffling off to lie down. She was thankful that the first trimester was nearly over. She'd been mildly ill when she was carrying Becca, but her queasiness had predictably dried up near the end of the third month.

Ira called her the following Friday. He came straight to the point. "Have you felt any better this week?"

Susannah was quick to reassure him. "There's been some improvement." *I'm only throwing up once a day instead of five times now.*

But Ira wasn't listening. "This has gone on long enough, Susannah. I want you to go to the doctor. I want you to hang up and call him right now."

She seized on the excuse like the lifeline it was. "His office hours are over for today. I'll have to wait till Monday."

"No way. This is an emergency, as far as I'm concerned."

"Ira, please, this is not abnormal. At my last checkup, the doctor wasn't concerned. I go in again in two weeks—"

"Susannah, I'm concerned about your health. Now either you call the doctor or I call Whit."

Susannah knew when to make a strategic retreat. "Listen, Ira, Becca's waking up. I have to go. I'll call you on Monday, okay? And *stop worrying.*"

The next day was Saturday. Becca was playing a boisterous game with several of her stuffed animals on the floor while Susannah dealt with yet another day of nausea. She was lying listlessly on the couch when the doorbell rang.

"Mom-mee! Doorbell ring!" Becca's habitually enthusiastic voice jarred Susannah out of the half doze she'd been in, and she sat up, groggy and disoriented. Putting a hand on the back of the couch, she prepared herself for the ordeal that occurred every time she lifted her head from a prone position.

Shuffling across the room, she peered through the peephole. She couldn't see anyone. That wasn't unusual. Myrna often stood to one side of the door. She opened the door with a smile plastered on her face. It faded to nothing when she saw Whit Montgomery standing in the hallway.

"Hello, Susannah." His baritone was as rich and pleasant to the ear as she'd remembered. When she simply stood and stared at him, he prompted, "May I come in?"

Dumbly she stepped aside. She didn't really invite him to enter, but he stepped past her anyway.

"*Whit!* Hi Whit, hi Whit, hi Whit." Becca turned the exuberant greeting into a high-decibel chant as she skidded to a halt in front of him. When he held out his arms, the tot didn't hesitate for even an instant before flinging herself forward.

As Whit's rich chocolate head bent over her daughter's own fair one and his arms lifted her into a bear hug, Susannah felt tears threaten. Life was so unfair. Becca needed a father. Someone who would love her as Whit was obviously prepared to love his own child.

She cleared her throat. "Um, Whit." When he turned with her child still cuddled in one big arm, she faltered for a minute, but self-preservation drove her onward. "I don't mean to be rude, but why are you here?"

For the briefest instant something fierce and furious flashed in the depths of his blue-black gaze. It was gone before Susannah could correctly interpret it, but the glimpse of a wilder side of this controlled man left her shaken. She prepared herself for a blast of anger.

"Two reasons." Whit's tone was so mild, she blinked. Had she imagined the tempest she'd witnessed in his gaze a moment ago?

He went on. "First, I've been wondering how Becca's getting along and I finally seized any excuse to see for myself." He raised his head from contemplation of Becca's rosy cheeks. "She looks one hundred percent improved to me."

"Oh, she is," Susannah assured him. "The doctor is delighted with her progress. In fact, she's fast becoming a real handful in an apartment of this size." She faltered under his steady regard. "What was the second reason?" she whispered.

Whit set Becca gently on the floor. Straightening again, he indicated the sofa. Becca dashed off to the bedroom to find Whit the Seal and they were alone when he turned to her. "Ira called me."

Susannah's eyes widened in shock. Ira did what? The nausea returned with a vengeance. She took deep breaths, but nothing helped. As her stomach revolted she ran headlong from the room.

She lingered in the bathroom for a long minute, trying to compose herself. How horribly embarrassing. If Ira had spoken with him, Whit knew how she'd been feeling. Besides, the man was far from stupid. He'd seen her do this same thing in the hospital. He'd be able to figure out the reason for her precipitous flight from the living room. As she placed her hand on the knob, it flew open from the other direction.

"Are you okay?" Whit looked panicked. His face relaxed a bit when he saw her standing quietly inside the door.
"Come lie down. We need to talk."

"About what?" She wasn't going to make this easy for
him. He and Ira had no right discussing her behind her
back. Besides, they both knew good and well it was her wish
that she not see Whit anymore. Ira, of all people,
should've understood that!

But when she saw the look in Whit's eyes, she allowed him
to lead her back to the sofa. She didn't resist even when he
pushed her down flat and perched on the edge, his hip
bumping intimately against hers.

"Susannah." Whit's voice was understated strained patience at its best. "I'm glad you're being so cautious about
this baby, but you can't jeopardize your own health." He
ruffled the hair of the little girl who'd returned to crawl up
in his lap. "You're needed by someone else, too."

She could hear the barely veiled worry in his voice.
"Whit, this is perfectly normal, as I told Ira. I'm almost at
the end of the first trimester. I've been feeling a bit better
every day. Soon I'll be fine."

"That's possible, but we're not waiting around for this
sickness to pack its bags and depart."

"We're not?" She had to ignore the feeling of warmth
that invaded her system at his use of the inclusive pronoun.

"Nope. I called the doctor before I came, and we're
meeting him at the office in half an hour."

Five

They were ushered right into an examination room at Dr. Bradley's office as soon as the nurse weighed her. Susannah was mildly surprised that Whit accompanied her into the room, but her stomach was too upset from the car ride for her to care very much. When Dr. Bradley entered in his usual quietly unflappable manner, Whit had helped Susannah up onto the examination table and she was breathing deeply, trying to settle her stomach.

"What seems to be the trouble today, Mrs. Taylor?" Dr. Bradley cordially shook hands with Whit, clearly assuming that he was her husband and that Becca, who'd been left in the nurse's care, was also his child.

"She's been extremely nauseated. Is it going to affect her health, or the baby's?" Whit jumped in before Susannah could open her mouth to answer Dr. Bradley.

Frowning down at her chart, the doctor said, "You've lost two more pounds since I saw you two weeks ago. Are you still experiencing vomiting?"

Susannah nodded.

"How frequently?"

When she told him, Whit stared at her. His scowl promised further discussion.

"We'll hope it soon fades away," the doctor said. "But, as I've told my patients a million times, every pregnancy is different. I've known ladies who were sick until the day they delivered."

"I can't endure this for six more months!" Susannah was horrified at the thought.

"No," agreed the doctor. "You certainly can't." He helped her lie back, then pulled up the bottom of her sweater a little bit and began to gently knead her stomach. "Now let's see if we can hear a heartbeat and then we'll decide what your options are."

"What do you mean, 'if'?" Whit looked stricken.

Dr. Bradley glanced at Whit, understanding his sudden panic. "Calm down, sir. We usually don't pick up the baby's heartbeat until the third or fourth month, so I haven't even tried to hear it until today. Mrs. Taylor's uterus appears to be growing normally despite her weight loss."

As the doctor gently but unceremoniously opened her pants down to the top of her pubic mound, Susannah could feel her fair skin coloring. Her gaze was drawn to Whit's face. He was staring at her, the hot blazing message in his eyes telling her that he was remembering every detail of their night together.

The doctor's next question destroyed what little composure she had left as he suddenly asked, "Are you still having a great deal of soreness in your breasts?"

"Yes." It was all she could do to get out the single word. She couldn't look at Whit again. An image of his dark head against her breast as he suckled the tender flesh streaked through her mind, and she flushed even more.

Dr. Bradley smeared a cold jellylike substance over her lower abdomen, then applied an instrument with a single round disk to the area. As he fiddled with the dials on the attached amplifier, Susannah could hear odd sounds, like ocean waves amid the background static. Dr. Bradley gently slid the instrument down to the right, and suddenly the room was filled with a rapid, staccato drumming sound pouring from the amplifier.

"There we go!" The doctor permitted himself a small smile of satisfaction. "Sounds as if your little one is doing just fine. Now all we have to do is get Mom straightened out." He reached for the amplifier.

"Wait!" Whit grabbed his wrist. "Is *that* my baby?" His voice was filled with awe.

Dr. Bradley grinned. "Yeah. That's your baby. Sounds like a lively little guy."

"Guy? You mean it's going to be a boy?" Whit sounded dazed.

"Sorry, I never make predictions. It was merely a figure of speech. Do you want a boy?" The room was shockingly silent when the doctor removed the instrument from Susannah's belly.

"I couldn't care less. I'll love either one."

Susannah forgot her embarrassment as she watched Whit's face soften. He really meant it, she could tell. She met his eyes with a tentative smile.

But he didn't smile back. He glowered at her.

She sighed. "Will you please relax?"

"Pardon?" The doctor glanced up from the notation he was entering on her chart.

"No." Whit's face was a mask of stone now.

The doctor chuckled as he helped Susannah to a sitting position. "He's going to watch you like a hawk," he told her with relish. Then he resumed his professional demeanor. "I want you off your feet completely for at least the next week. I'm considering admitting you to the hospital."

"Dr. Bradley!" Susannah was aghast. "I can't go to the hospital. I have a two-year-old and a job to worry about—"

"Mrs. Taylor. This is merely a precaution. You appear to be crossing the hurdle, but you've lost a lot of weight—" he consulted his chart "—twelve pounds altogether. You need to take it easy. Rest and relaxation for a week. The following week, you can get up for short periods, but you should still get a lot of rest. Take it very easy until you come in for your next checkup. Then we'll see where we stand."

Tears welled in Susannah's eyes. She hated the sign of weakness, but she was so shocked. Never had she expected to have such difficulties after an easy first pregnancy. "Is there any way I could avoid being hospitalized?" she asked quietly.

"Only if you agree to go home and stay in bed for a minimum of one week. You can use the bathroom and that's it."

Tears rolled down Susannah's cheeks. "All right."

Whit moved to her side and placed a hard arm around her. "She'll listen." His voice held a hint of steel that Susannah had never heard before.

Dr. Bradley's eyes danced with mirth. "I'll expect a telephone call from you every day this week with a report."

When Susannah awoke in her bed several hours later, the nausea had subsided. Carefully she got to her feet and was gratified when she was able to go to the kitchen and eat a slice of toast and drink a glass of milk. Just as she finished and set her dishes in the sink, a key scraped in her door and Whit came striding in with Becca riding triumphantly on his shoulders.

He stopped dead when he saw her. "What are you doing out of bed?"

"I only got up to eat," Susannah said reasonably.

"You can have your meals in bed until next week. The doctor said bed rest and he meant it."

They glared at each other in stubborn silence for a long minute. Finally Susannah sighed. "All right. I give—this time."

She walked back to bed in a huffy silence. Becca came scampering in a moment later, clutching a pile of books. "Mom-mee read 'tories?"

"Mommy would love to read stories," Susannah said as Becca scrambled up on the bed and snuggled in beside her. She read all the books one time through, savoring the special chore she'd felt too ill to enjoy for the past several weeks. At Becca's request, they were starting over when Whit came to the door.

"We need to talk," he announced.

Susannah merely stared at him. She still felt disgruntled about the way he'd taken over her life today. She wanted him to know it wasn't going to happen again.

"Myrna has dinner ready for Becca." Whit hesitated, his deep blue eyes unreadable. "Could I please speak with you while Becca's eating?"

Susannah relented. He was making an effort not to be offensive. "I suppose so." Uncomfortable with the idea of being alone in her bedroom with Whit, she began to slide from the bed.

"No, stay there." His voice stayed her efforts. "Remember what the doctor said?"

Picking Becca up with an easy grace, he walked from the room. Susannah could hear him teasing the little girl as he delivered her to Myrna.

Then he was back, striding into the room and perching on the edge of the bed before she could protest. His thigh slid along the length of her body, resting warmly against her.

Susannah hitched her body away from the searing contact, cursing the fair complexion she knew had colored.

Whit gave her a thoughtful look, but the anger she'd seen earlier was nowhere in evidence. "Have you thought about what you'll do now?"

Susannah pleated the quilt between her fingers, grimacing. "I guess I'll have to ask Ira for more time off. And ask Myrna to help me with Becca a bit longer." She stopped, hating the idea of being indebted so deeply to other people whom she could never hope to adequately repay.

"Yes, but what about meals and cleaning and all the other little things that need to be done on a daily basis?"

Susannah looked at the floor rather than meet his eyes. "I'm sure I can manage for a week. I'll feel better soon, and Dr. Bradley said I could get up after that."

"Susannah, you cannot get out of this bed to do anything for the remainder of the week. And even after that, you need to take it easy." Whit's voice was firm, and she caught again that hint of the steel she'd detected in the doctor's office earlier.

"What do you suggest I do?" Her snappish demand was rhetorical; she didn't really expect an answer. Suddenly she decided there was no reason to hide her financial condition from him if it would keep him from hounding her any more. "I have hospital bills coming out my ears, a child and a home to maintain. I don't have the money to hire even temporary help."

She'd dropped her death grip on the quilt to wave her hands in the air as she spoke. Whit captured them and gently returned them to the bed, holding her small palms within his rough, callused fingers. He looked at their joined hands as he responded to her irritated statement.

"Actually, I do have a suggestion." He held up a hand when she would've interrupted him, and Susannah subsided. "You need someone to care for Becca, as well as someone to pamper you for a week or so. This baby is more my responsibility than yours. Would you consider coming to stay on Turtle Island for a while?"

Susannah opened her mouth. She closed it again. When she opened it to tell him that would be insane, he put his hand over her lips. She quieted instantly as her body responded to the feel of that hard palm brushing her sensitive lips. The contact increased her awareness of his big, muscled frame so very near to hers in the secluded bedroom.

"I have a couple who work for me. I believe I told you that before. They could be a big help with Becca."

She must be sicker than she'd thought, Susannah decided. She was actually considering the idea. "But...we agreed not to have any more contact...." Her voice trailed away.

"And we don't have to after you're back on your feet," Whit soothed her. "It's just for a short time." He gave her an impudent grin. It creased his cheeks into attractive dimples and displayed flashing white teeth. Its charm hit her like a hard blow straight to the solar plexus, stealing her breath. "You might as well say yes, because otherwise I'll be forced to camp on your sofa until I'm convinced you're healthy again."

He'd expected to have to beg, he reflected silently as he maneuvered the boat alongside the dock just before sunset that evening. While he'd played with Becca in the park, he'd marshaled a half dozen logical arguments to convince Susannah that a short-term visit to his home would be the most reasonable course of action to solve her problems.

He'd never gotten the chance to air them.

She'd given him a long, considering stare after he'd reinforced his sincerity with the stupid statement about staying with her if she wouldn't come. He could almost see her gathering her energy to throw him out of her home. And her life.

But she hadn't. He'd nearly whooped aloud when she'd opened her mouth and quietly said, "I guess we could do that. Just for a week or so."

He'd been badly shaken this morning when she'd opened the door and he'd seen how thin she was. He'd realized then just how much he was coming to want this child. Keeping an eye on its mother until he was sure she was back on her feet was the sensible thing to do. That was the only reason he'd proposed this visit.

Axel was waiting, as Whit had known he would be. Hilda was probably up at the house in a frenzy of last-minute cleaning, he thought. They'd both been shocked when he'd called them and told them to prepare rooms for a woman and a small child. He guessed he'd have to sit them down and explain the situation to them after his guests were settled tonight.

Ira'd been only slightly less flabbergasted when Whit had called him.

"This is more than just satisfying the terms of the will, isn't it?" He was a shrewd lawyer.

"Only because I want this baby. And if I have to keep a close eye on Susannah to get it, then I will."

"Good luck." Ira had sounded amused once he'd absorbed Whit's determination. "Something tells me I may not see Susannah again for a while. She's a damned good receptionist. Tell her I'll hold her job for her until after the baby comes if she needs to be off that long."

Docking the launch, Whit threw the lines to Axel and turned, striding back along the deck to where Becca sat.

"Ready to go see my house, punkin?" He held out his arms to the tot, whose gilt hair gleamed pale gold in the evening sun.

"Mom-mee come, too." Becca came to him, but she was clearly anxious to see her mother near her side.

"Mommy's coming, too." He leaped lightly to the deck with Becca in his arms.

"Axel, this is Becca Taylor. Her mother is our other guest." He handed Becca to Axel, pleased when the little girl didn't pucker up. "Let me go get your mommy, Becca."

Stepping back on board, Whit entered the small cabin where Susannah had promised she would rest until he came to get her. He found her lying on the single bunk.

"Okay, Sleeping Beauty, your turn to meet the wilds."

Susannah sat up. "I wasn't sleeping. I'm dying to get up, but I promised . . ." She gave an exaggerated sigh.

Whit felt his lips quiver. "That's right. You did." He stepped forward and lifted her into his arms. "Come on, I'll introduce you to Axel and my home."

Susannah clutched at him. "Whit! I can walk. Put me down."

Whit merely laughed. "Nope. The doctor doesn't want you on your feet, so you're stuck with me." She felt good in his arms, light and so fragile, and he was struck again by how little this pregnancy had changed her thus far. Her hair brushed against his cheek as he ducked his head to exit the cabin. He inhaled deeply of the fragrance it carried, and he was abruptly catapulted back in time to the night he'd carried her to a bed. That unique fragrance, not perfume but her own special woman's scent, had drifted around them then.

His feet slowed on the steps.

Alerted to his change of pace, Susannah looked up at him with wide, questioning eyes.

He stopped completely, drinking in the wavy spill of her hair over his shoulder, her porcelain features, the violet eyes shadowed with puzzlement, her softly parted lips—he was riveted to those lips, unable to look away as the dying sun caught the sheen of moisture left from the last pass of her tongue and turned her mouth into a gleaming invitation. Would she let him kiss her? The thought of meeting her tongue with his own caused erotic explosions inside his body, and he could feel the stirring flesh of his loins growing, pulsing to rigid life.

Susannah went still in his arms and he knew she was as aware of him as he'd become of her. Her eyes darkened and her pink tongue came out to slide slowly over her full bottom lip, leaving even more moisture behind. Her gaze was locked on his as he lowered his head, drawn by the promises her soft skin offered.

Instants before contact became inevitable, a piping voice from outside called, "Mom-mee? Mom-mee coming?" Susannah stiffened reflexively, awareness flashing into her gaze. Although she didn't turn from him, the spell was broken. Disappointment flooded his system.

Determined not to let awkwardness between them frighten her away before she'd experienced his life-style, Whit continued to lower his head. Hugging her close, he whispered against her ear. "Welcome to Turtle Island."

Resuming his steps, he carried her up on deck, taking her right to the Jeep in which her daughter waited. Becca snuggled happily against Susannah when Whit placed her in the vehicle. Pausing to introduce Axel, Whit started the motor and drove up the rude crushed-shell road toward the house.

"Goodness! What a rough ride," Susannah chattered through her teeth.

Glancing over at her, Whit had to grin. "Relax. This is like riding a horse. The stiffer you sit, the worse it gets. Let your body move with the bumps. You should be glad Axel isn't driving. I never ride with him if I can avoid it."

"Is this the only means of transportation on the island?" Susannah was looking out at the heavy undergrowth on her side of the road with interest.

"We have a number of bicycles, but other than that, we generally walk unless we need this to transport something." Whit was encouraged by her interest.

"What would you be transporting?"

Whit shrugged. "We get groceries and supplies once a month. That's always a big load to haul up to the house. When I have large quantities of nest-protection equipment, I'll make a run down to the other end of the island and drop it off for the teams who are working, but we often carry it in smaller loads on the bikes. There's also the infrequent time when I might have to transport a turtle or some other large animal." He laughed. "And believe me, we're grateful for the Jeeps then!"

"You have wild animals on this island?"

He could hear the apprehension in Susannah's voice, and he hastened to reassure her. "No big carnivores. I was referring to a few times that wounded manatees have drifted in. We contact the guys down at Sea World who have a good reputation for rehabilitating them if they can be saved. They come up and get them, but I usually move them to a protected bay on the other side of the island where the sharks can't get at them. Even then, we usually tow them or float them in a half-submerged boat, but an all-terrain vehicle is the fastest way to get between points in an emergency.''

Susannah looked thoughtful. ''Are there any dangers I need to know about, Whit? I can't take chances with Becca.''

''There are a few hazards,'' Whit allowed. ''We have a hard-and-fast rule about swimming here. The only place anyone swims is in the bay I told you about, and then only in broad daylight with a buddy. Mama turtles are an easy mark for sharks. There are always a few around. I can't take chances with all the students who are under my supervision. Also, there are several types of poisonous snakes around. They don't ordinarily come up near the house. Axel keeps the lawn and bushes trimmed closely to discourage them.''

''What kind of poisonous snakes?'' Susannah's voice was neutral. Whit couldn't tell what she might be thinking.

''Cottonmouth moccasins and diamondback rattlers, mostly. A few coral snakes and copperheads, too. Nobody's been bitten in my lifetime, though. They're as scared of us as we are of them and cautious procedures have paid off.''

''Anything else?''

''Not really. Once in a great while we're visited by a 'gator that wanders away from the mainland, but they're not indigenous to the island and I call the Department of Natural Resources to come take them home.'' He pointed through the bug-smeared windshield of the vehicle. ''Look up ahead. We're nearly there.''

Susannah obediently focused her attention on the view unfolding as the vehicle came out of the trees.

Whit surveyed it with the same feeling of pride it always gave him. This time, though, his thoughts were edged with awareness of Susannah. What did she think of his home?

The narrow shell road between scrub pines and dense undergrowth abruptly emerged at the edge of a rolling lawn dotted by flowering crabapple, redbud and wild plum trees. Camellias, poinsettias and roses were grouped around the circle that fronted his home and in beds bordering the first floor.

The big house stood amid the lengthening shadows of evening, the setting sun reflected in its many windows. Of rose-hued brick, it was an imposing two-story complete with a columned portico fronting the house.

Whit drove directly up to the entrance. The shelled pathway extended right to the steps in front of the door. As he jumped out and strode around to help his guests from the vehicle, the front door opened and a big woman stood framed in the glow from the interior.

Susannah sat numbly in the Jeep. She'd never realized Whit was rich! The Mercedes should've been a clue, she conceded, but even that hadn't prepared her for *this!* The huge house mocked her even as she admired its beauty.

When he'd told her about his family's island, she'd pictured a tiny hill jutting out of the sea to which his home clung like a stubborn barnacle. Instead he owned a piece of prime real estate nearly five miles long and half as wide. And the house! The house was a masterpiece of Georgian architecture that looked as old as the island itself, although superbly maintained. Just how long had Whit's family owned this land? Susannah wondered. There were some obvious concessions to recent technological advances, such as the satellite dish neatly camouflaged by shrubbery that was set on the lawn, the tightly sealed storm windows, and the hum of an air-conditioning system, but the overall impression was that of age. Solid, well-heeled ancient tradition.

Whit came around to the side of the automobile and held
out his arms to Becca as Susannah took in even more detail. But Becca had been overwhelmed by the loud, rough
ride, and when Whit extended his arms, she wailed and
buried her face in Susannah's lap. "Mom-mee! 'Tay wif
Mom-mee!"

Susannah came back to earth with an abrupt thud.
Shelving her misgivings about the way Whit had omitted
certain details of his life-style, she concentrated on the crying child.

"Here, Becca. Mommy's coming, too. You let Whit help
you out and then Mommy will get out."

Becca shook her head and cried even more piteously.
"No! Mom-mee, too."

Susannah looked at Whit, registering the dismay on his
features. Too bad. This was his idea, after all. "I'm open to
suggestions."

Much to her surprise, he rose to the challenge without
blinking an eyelash. "Let's do this the easy way. You hold
her, and I'll take you both."

Becca had already climbed into Susannah's lap and
wound her thin arms around her mother's neck, but Susannah was dubious. "I don't think you could carry us both.
Why don't I—"

But once again Whit pre-empted her speech with the simple method of hoisting her into his arms. This time, of
course, Becca was snuggled under Susannah's chin, but the
feeling was still sinfully exciting. She'd never been carried
anywhere before she met him and it was strangely enjoy-
able. For an instant she wished Becca weren't there, and that
the stranger on the threshold would disappear so that Whit
could kiss her as he'd nearly done on the narrow steps of his
boat. The sanity returned. This was merely a practical arrangement, she reminded herself. As Whit carried her up the
stairs, the cool assessment in the eyes of the big woman
blocking the doorway brought the message home forcibly.
She was a guest, no more.

"Hilda, this is Susannah Taylor, and her daughter, Becca. Ladies, my housekeeper, cook and first love, Hilda Hewitt."

The sharp brown eyes under the scraped-back bun of steel-gray hair softened at his last words. "I practically raised this boy," Hilda informed them. Susannah wondered if the statement was a warning or motherly fondness. The woman's next words were addressed to Whit. "Can't she walk?"

"Of course she can walk." Whit laughed as though Hilda's question wasn't rude and impertinent. "But I enjoy carrying her."

"Huh." The snort was a statement in itself.

"Hilda..." Whit hesitated, looking almost regretful for an instant. "Susannah is pregnant. She's been sick." He began to walk up a flight of wide, curving stairs, still holding her.

"Robert Whittier Montgomery the Fifth, you wait just one minute!" Hilda charged up the stairs behind them. "Pregnant?"

"Yup." The strange look he'd worn was gone, and he was wearing a puckish grin. His tone was full of pride.

"And I suppose it's yours."

Whit looked at Susannah. "Is it mine?"

Susannah was speechless. This was without doubt the most bizarre conversation she'd ever heard in her entire life. Recovering her composure, she gave him a look that should've shriveled him to dust. "That doesn't deserve a response."

Whit threw back his head and laughed. He seemed oddly relaxed and less constrained than Susannah had ever seen him. His island definitely agreed with him.

"Sorry." His grin looked anything but. He looked over his shoulder at Hilda. "Of course, it's mine. Why else would I be bringing her here?"

Six

_____

"I'm sorry." The words sounded a little rusty, so Whit repeated them. The phrase echoed in the silence of the big kitchen. Hilda took off her reading glasses and carefully marked her place in the cookbook she'd been perusing. Axel laid down the sharp knife beside the little wooden turtle he'd half finished carving. Whit felt ashamed as he met the bewildered gazes of the couple whom he'd known since childhood. He'd avoided this task because he dreaded trying to explain his actions to them. Now he had to contend with rightfully hurt feelings, as well. "I've been meaning to tell you," he began. "But it isn't the easiest thing in the world to say—"

"Hell," Axel growled. "It ain't our place to judge you. You're a healthy one 'n' we know it ain't easy livin' out here all alone. These things happen, boy."

"Not quite like this." Whit was touched. They'd obviously agreed to give him the benefit of the doubt. He searched for the right words. "I—we—did this on purpose."

He could see from their shocked expressions that he'd surprised them even more. "Are you married to that little gal?" Hilda was confused now.

"No. And I don't plan to be, either. Do you remember when Ira Hanrahan called after Granddad died?"

When both nodded, Whit went on to tell them about the unusual terms of his inheritance, and his creative solution. They knew that if the island were sold, it would be developed faster than a turtle could get tangled in a shrimper's net.

Hilda's face registered distress when he'd finished telling them the outline of the contract upon which he and Susannah had agreed. "What kind of woman could walk away from her own child?"

Whit was silent. He'd asked himself that very question a million times in recent days. At first he'd assumed she was just a greedy bitch, a money-hungry career woman, but after coming to know her, seeing her with her child, it was becoming impossible to cling to that comforting rationale. Susannah was warm, feminine, *vulnerable.* He'd seen too much evidence that she'd needed the money to make it through Becca's surgery. He wasn't naive. He knew insurance only covered the tip of the iceberg in cases such as Becca's.

"I don't know," he finally offered quietly. "But I can tell you, this isn't easy for her. Not physically, and not emotionally."

Susannah awoke early. For the briefest minute she wondered where she was, then memories of yesterday leaked into her mind. Taking her time, she examined the room Hilda had readied for her.

It was obviously a woman's room. Wallpapered in a charming pale pink, rose and lavender flower pattern, a carpet of lush rose covered the floor. Heavy rose draperies of the same deep shade were caught back at the long windows, exposing lacy sheers beneath. One window sported a window seat that was upholstered in a fabric to match the walls and strewn with complementary pillows of various shapes, lavishly embellished with lace and ribbon. A wardrobe, four-poster and vanity were all of the same suite. The flowers in an elegant crystal bowl gracing the top of the vanity added a final touch of wealth and elegance to the room.

Remembering the events of yesterday, she wondered what in the world she'd gotten herself into. She must've been temporarily deranged to agree to Whit's plan to stay on Turtle Island. Even a week seemed forever. This place was unbelievably remote. Oh well. She was confined to this room for the duration, anyway. They might just manage to survive until Whit took them back to civilization next Saturday.

Only seven days away.

It couldn't come too soon. She tried to ignore the little voice that mocked, *But then you won't be seeing Whit again. Are you sure that's what you want?*

The heavy door from the hallway creaked once in warning before it opened unceremoniously. Becca darted into the room in her pajamas, shouting, "Mom-mee!"

Whit was right behind her. "Shh, Becca, Mommy might be sleeping."

"It's all right. Mommy's wide awake." Susannah carefully pulled the covers high over her sheer eyelet nightgown, averting her gaze from the sight of Whit clad in a T-shirt and walking shorts. It didn't help. The same nervous sensation that always attacked her system when she was near him struck again, heightened by the intimacy created by having him walk into her bedroom before breakfast. It wasn't helped any by the two muscular, hair-covered legs that stopped at the edge of her vision, demanding a more thorough appraisal. She held out her arms as Becca scrambled up onto the bed, using the child as an excuse to avoid his eyes.

"Whit take Bec-ca beat-th," the child announced.

Susannah looked blank. Without a frame of reference, it was sometimes difficult to follow Becca's conversations. Before Susannah could ask her to repeat her words, Becca pushed her way out of Susannah's arms and climbed off the bed again. As she raced down the hallway, she shouted, "Me get book-th!"

Susannah shook her head, smiling ruefully at Whit. "Where does she want you to take her?"

"I offered to take her down to the beach after breakfast," Whit translated. "If you don't object."

She dredged up a smile and shook her head. "Of course I don't object. I'm very grateful that you'd take time out of your day for Becca. You certainly aren't obligated to entertain her. The beach will be a real treat for her." Then her face clouded. "This will be the first time she's really had the chance to explore a beach. I wish I could be there."

Chagrin chased itself across Whit's tanned features. "I'm sorry," he offered with real regret. "I never thought that you'd like to share these firsts with her."

"It's okay," Susannah reassured him quickly. "I'll walk down soon, and she can show me all the treasures she's found."

"Not until after you see Dr. Bradley."

She arched one delicately curved eyebrow. "He said a week," she reminded Whit. "Saturday is one week."

"After your checkup." Whit's voice was adamant.

"I'm not an invalid." Susannah was trying hard to hang onto her temper.

Whit came across to the side of the bed. When he planted his hands on his hips, her eyes were drawn to the way his shorts stretched across jutting hipbones and quiescent masculinity. "You are under a doctor's care," he gritted. "I want this baby. If I have to tie you to that bed to get it, that's exactly what I'll do."

Susannah struggled with her rising anger, despite the breathlessness his nearness evoked. Suddenly the image of herself bound and gagged and tied to the bed in this elegant room rose in her head. She stared hard at Whit, biting her lip. It didn't work. A giggle escaped.

Whit scowled. "That was funny?"

"I just . . ." She had to pause and chuckle. "I just had a vision of me, with a huge round tummy, tied to this bed, with Hilda coming in to deliver my daily ration of bread and water."

Whit shook his head. He didn't smile, but she could see his tension had eased. "That's some imagination you've got."

He looked down at her for a moment longer, and some emotion she couldn't define passed over his face, his deep-sea eyes alight with . . . Whit cleared his throat and the moment was gone. "Um, I'll carry you downstairs after I come back from the beach, if you like. You could spend part of the day on a lounge."

"That would be wonderful!" Susannah was touched by his thoughtfulness. "This room is beautiful, but I wasn't looking forward to being confined to it for a whole week. Who does it belong to?"

Whit's face changed. His eyes became lumps of hard sapphire. "It was my mother's room."

"Oh! I don't want to take your mother's room—"

"She hasn't used it since she left when I was four years old. You aren't displacing anyone, so don't worry about it."

Silence fell between them. Questions were swirling through Susannah's head like a turning kaleidoscope. Why had his mother left? Why hadn't she taken him with her? Had she ever come back? But she didn't ask any of them. The look in Whit's eyes warned her that the topic was taboo.

She merely said, "It's a lovely room."

"Right. By the way, I have something for you." Whit turned and vanished through the doorway against which he'd been leaning.

Before she could give herself time to reconsider, Susannah called him back. "Whit?"

"What?" He reappeared again.

"Where does that door go? What's on the other side?"

A glint of humor lit his eyes. "My bedroom." And he was gone again, leaving Susannah to stare at the empty doorway in dumbfounded silence.

He was back again before she'd regained her voice, tossing a book down beside her on the bed. "I thought if you hadn't brought anything along to kill time, you might enjoy reading this. It's written by a prominent naturalist who's studied turtles. I think it's one of the best books about turtles a layman can read."

Susannah fingered the book, smiling a little as she noted the picture of the big sea turtle crawling down to the breakers that graced the cover. "Thanks." But her next words echoed the thoughts rolling around in her head like storm-brewed waves. "Why am I in a room that connects to yours?"

Whit continued to stare at the book she was lightly rubbing with her forefinger. "Hilda put you in here without consulting me. I guess she thought you were—we were—engaged in a relationship that necessitated us being in close proximity."

Susannah knew the damning color was rising in her face again. She felt as if she spent most of her time in Whit's company trying not to blush. "Perhaps you should have another room prepared."

Whit shrugged. "I thought this might be practical after I mulled it over. If you need anything in the night, you can call me. And I don't want to make more work for Hilda if this is suitable." His logic was flimsy, but Susannah did hate to burden the older woman with unnecessary work. Who would ever know?

That one was easy to answer. She would. She'd be able to hear him moving around and she'd imagine him taking off his clothes, baring that magnificent body, the muscles rippling in his arms and down across the washboard ridges of his taut stomach— Stop it, Susannah!

Resolutely she picked up the book, avoiding his gaze. "All right. I guess I'll see you after you take Becca to the beach."

Time passed faster than she'd anticipated. Soon the day of her next exam arrived. After breakfast, Whit came into Susannah's bedroom where she was reading to Becca. His dark head was damp and she realized he must've just showered. His short-sleeved shirt clung to firm muscles, and Susannah lowered her head to her daughter before he could see the appreciation in her eyes.

"Reading again! Do you like stories?" he teased Becca.

"Bec-ca like 'tories," she told him solemnly.

"You can never read to a child too much." Susannah put on her best lecture tone. "Reading aloud stimulates language development. Young children learn primarily by imitation, and providing them with a wide expanse of read-aloud literature enhances intellectual development in a way nothing else can."

Whit laughed. "You sound just like a book I bought recently. I couldn't agree more. I'm planning to read at least six stories a day to my child."

Susannah tried not to wince at the mention of the baby. "That's an admirable goal. Pair that with actual experiences and a child will be light-years ahead of the average kindergartner by the time he's school age."

"I forgot you were trained as a teacher."

"*Nearly* trained as a teacher." Susannah stressed the adverb. "I'll probably always regret that impulsive decision to leave school." Afraid her voice would convey all the despair she felt at the folly of that long-ago choice, she looked away from him. If only she'd finished her student teaching and gotten her degree! A good teaching job would've offered much more security for a single parent, not to mention the insurance that would've helped ease her through Becca's illness after Steve left. Then she would never have been forced to act as a surrogate for a man who was looking forward to the day when he could claim her baby. The man to whom she was growing all too attached, despite her initial reservations about his unusual life-style.

He must have sensed her distress because he hurried to change the subject.

"It's nearly time to go if we don't want to be late for the doctor's appointment. Are you all ready?"

"Hilda has everything packed and waiting in the hallway."

"Not anymore. I already took it down to the dock so Axel could load it. All that's left is you."

"Okay." She turned to Becca, sitting quietly beside her. "Well, punkin, are you ready to go home?"

Much to her dismay, Becca burst into tears.

"What's wrong? Does something hurt?" Almost frantic, she pulled up the loose shirt Becca wore and examined the neatly healing incision that formed a T in the center of her chest.

Whit knelt beside the bed, looking as worried as Susannah. "Tell us what's wrong, Becca." At the sound of his voice, Becca unexpectedly flung herself toward him, sobbing wildly. Susannah made a grab for her, but Whit caught the tiny girl as she hurled herself at him. Becca wound her arms around his neck tightly while Whit and Susannah stared at each other in puzzled concern.

"Baby, tell Mommy what's wrong." After the first frightened reaction, Susannah didn't believe Becca was in physical distress. Her fears were confirmed when she tried to take Becca from Whit's arms. Becca howled even more loudly and locked her arms around his neck. "No, Mommee!" Becca let go of Whit long enough to slap blindly at her mother's hands. "Me 'tay. No go. 'Tay Whit go

beat-th.'' Her words were even harder to understand than
normal, punctuated by screams and hiccuping sobs.

Susannah sighed. She should've seen this coming.
''Becca,'' she began. ''We had a nice visit with Whit, but
now we have to go home. Whit's too busy to take care of us
all the time.''

Her arguments had no discernible effect on the child, who
continued to wail out her demands at the top of her lungs.
''Bec-ca 'tay. Hep Hil'a. Me like Whit-th houth!''

''I know you like Whit's house. I like Whit's house, too.
But don't you like our house? All your toys will be lonely
without you.'' That was desperation speaking, and from the
glimmer of amusement in Whit's eye, he knew it.

Still supporting the clinging tot, he raised his head and
looked for a long, measured moment at Susannah before
opening his mouth to speak. ''You don't have to go, you
know.'' His voice was quiet, but his eyes were sincere. ''I'd
love to have you stay, and to be honest, I'd feel better if you
had help for a while until we're sure you're feeling good
again. I know you aren't comfortable imposing on your
neighbor indefinitely.''

Susannah began to shake her head, but he held up a hand.
''Becca's so happy here. You don't have room for her to explore and run around in your apartment. I think she looks
terrific after a week of sea air. Just think how a month or so
would improve her condition.''

Susannah frowned at his blatant maneuvering, but her
heart wasn't in it. She wanted to be here, there was no use
lying to herself. Just as she knew deep down that the reason
she'd allowed him to talk her into this in the first place
wasn't because of any of the logical arguments he'd presented. On the contrary, the powerful sexual attraction he
held for her, when combined with his easygoing, affection-
ate nature, was the clincher. They were an irresistible com-
bination to a woman who'd known neither. Great basis for
a rational decision, she admonished herself.

Aloud, she said, "Ira will be expecting me back at work soon. I couldn't stay if I wanted to."

A strange expression crossed Whit's face. Then he admitted, "I've already talked with Ira about extending your leave. He'll hold your job until after the baby comes if you need him to."

"Until after the baby comes!" Susannah was astonished. "I can't possibly take that much time off."

"Why not?"

"For one thing, I have bills to pay. How do you expect me to manage that without an income?"

"If you're living out here, you won't have any expenses except the maintenance on your apartment," Whit argued. "You don't have to pay for food or utilities, and you won't have car expenses because you won't be driving."

"It's out of the question. I can't—"

Her eyes widened as Whit put his hand over her mouth, stifling her hasty words. "At least think about it until after the doctor sees you," he urged. "Give it some serious consideration before you say no."

One hour later Dr. Bradley looked over the tops of his glasses at Susannah. "Were you planning to go back to work any time soon, Mrs. Taylor?"

"I'd hoped to," Susannah began tentatively.

"But she certainly doesn't need to," Whit inserted.

"Good." Dr. Bradley made no bones about his relief. He smiled kindly at Susannah, but his words were addressed to Whit. "I'd like to see her get more rest throughout this pregnancy."

"Then she'll continue to take it easy." Whit felt like shouting his delight. Now he could convince her to come back to the island!

"Is there a reason why no one's asking my opinion?" Susannah sounded slightly peeved.

"Yes," Whit told her firmly. "Because you don't listen to anyone's advice, anyway. You aren't getting a choice."

* * *

While Susannah entertained Becca and directed, Whit packed everything she'd need for a longer-term stay on the island. She'd suggested they stay the night and finish it in the morning, but Whit was determined to get them back onto Turtle Island before darkness fell. In some illogical part of his mind, he was afraid that if Susannah didn't come today, she never would.

Why was it so important to have her there? He gave himself any number of reasonable answers. She needed to take it easy if she weren't going to lose the baby. He wanted to be able to see how her pregnancy progressed, to share these early days of bonding with his child. The research he'd been reading highlighted how vital it was for a fetus to hear its father's voice while still in utero. He'd feel silly explaining that to Susannah, so he'd concentrated on points she would accept. Becca was doing wonderfully. Her color had improved, and each day they went down to the beach, she was able to run a little farther.

But he didn't voice his real thoughts. He didn't understand them himself. He could picture Susannah in his home in a way no other woman had ever fit. Not even Marguerite.

Marguerite. He hadn't thought of her in a long time. As he helped Susannah onto the dock, he couldn't help but compare the two women. Physically, they couldn't have been more different. Marguerite was tall where Susannah was petite, though both were slim with just the right amount of curves. Marguerite had been dark-haired, with flashing black eyes that could sparkle with amusement or flame with fury—often within a ten-second span. She'd been moody and unpredictable. If he hadn't been so overwhelmed by the rampant sexuality she exuded and practiced on him every chance she got, he'd have realized a lot sooner that she'd never adjust to life on an isolated island. Marguerite loved parties, dinners, dancing. Marguerite couldn't exist without dozens of phone calls to her girlfriends every day, without weekly jaunts to the beauty parlor, the health spa and the exclusive stores she loved to patronize.

Susannah wasn't really moody or unpredictable, he thought. She was a hard one to figure out, though. He'd never met a woman who was so quiet. Often he wondered what was going on behind those opaque violet eyes.

She didn't look a thing like Marguerite. Funny, he wouldn't have thought she could turn him on the same way, either. If he were honest, it wasn't the same at all. Marguerite had been about as subtle as a Sherman tank, flaunting her body until a man was so hot the results were almost a foregone conclusion. And Marguerite hadn't been shy about using her long-fingered hands to produce a desired reaction, either.

He almost smiled at the notion of Susannah being that bold. She'd die first. But no question about it, she turned him on every time he drew a breath. He'd almost swear he was tuned in to her smell. All she had to do was walk into a room and his body rose as predictably as a balloon attached to a helium tank. She'd looked like absolute living hell when he'd knocked at her door that day, but his body hadn't even noticed that she was colorless with her hair hanging in limp tangles. All he'd been able to do was fight the sexual heat she radiated with needle-sharp reminders of why he was involved with her in the first place. She was giving up a baby. For money. His money. And he'd do well to remember it, to keep her at arm's length.

His resolve lasted a whole two hours. He'd taken Susannah's and Becca's belongings to their respective rooms and wished them both a good evening. Then he'd gone to the kitchen to inform Hilda that they'd be staying for an indefinite period of time.

Now he sat in his study, with its view of the silvered ocean surging onto the beaches where turtles would soon be coming ashore. He had a ledger open in front of him and was supposed to be reconciling the accounts, but his mind was on the woman sleeping just a single floor above him.

The knock on the door snapped his head away from the window. Hilda and Axel rarely bothered him after dark; they usually retired to their own apartment at dusk. "Come in."

When the knob turned and the door silently swung inward, Susannah stood there. He drank in every detail of her appearance, from the gilt hair floating around her shoulders, down over the sensible cotton robe she wore to the tips of bare feet peeking from under the hem.

"I'm sorry to bother you," she began without preamble.

"That's okay. I wasn't having much luck concentrating anyhow." *I was thinking of you.* When she continued to stand in the doorway, he got to his feet and came around the desk to the leather wingback chairs grouped around a sturdy masculine coffee table in front of a small hearth. "Have a seat."

Silently she picked her way across the thick carpet, perching on the very edge of one of the unyielding chairs. Her gaze darted around the room, avoiding contact with his. Whit watched her covertly as he took a seat across from her. Something was making her edgy. He waited, but still she didn't volunteer a reason for her unexpected visit.

Finally he said, "Is there a problem, Susannah?"

She started, looking fully at him for the first time since she'd entered the room. "Oh, no. I just wanted to tell you...I mean, I thought you'd like to know—oh, never mind!" She began to rise from her chair.

Whit thought she was adorable when she got flustered. He reached out and grabbed her arm as she swished by him. "Wait."

She stopped beside his chair but still wouldn't look at him. Without releasing her wrist, he slowly stood until he was facing her in the dim room. Just the simple act of touching her smooth skin had his pulse beating faster. The lamp on his desk cast a golden glow over half her face as she looked up at him; the other half was shadowed. The same light silhouetted the gentle curve of her breast beneath the cotton robe and below the belted waist; he could see the faintest suggestion of a bulge, the first sign of his child growing within her he'd been able to detect.

"How are you feeling?" He asked the question simply because he didn't know what else to say to her.

"Fine. The queasiness is gone. My hormones must be settling down." She almost smiled, and although it wasn't a come-on, Whit felt his body respond to the expression and to her choice of words. His hormones were certainly going wild right now.

As he searched for something else to say, Susannah stepped into the uncomfortable silence. "I wanted to tell you I've been feeling movement."

"Movement?" It took a minute for her words to sink in.

"The baby. Remember?" She did smile this time. A gentle warmth lit the side of her face illuminated by the light.

Whit was suddenly intensely interested in every word she uttered. "When did you first notice it?"

"A week ago. I wanted to be sure before I mentioned it."

"You weren't sure you felt the baby moving?" He'd assumed that once the baby got active, the mother would know right away.

"Not at first. It feels like tiny flutters, as if your insides are shifting into a more comfortable position. Even when you've been through this before, you're never quite sure if they're what you think they are. But they're a bit stronger this week, more like someone put their hands in a pool and stirred up little waves."

Whit's gaze was drawn to her stomach. "Would I be able to feel anything?"

Susannah shook her head. "Not yet. In another month, maybe." She hesitated. "If I'm still here, you can feel him for yourself."

Whit smiled down at her. He had every intention of keeping her here until the baby came. "I'd like that. Very much."

Susannah gazed up at him, searching his eyes. He wondered what she'd do, what she'd say, if he dropped his head and closed the distance between her lips and his. If he ran his tongue across the seam of those bowed lips, would she open them and let him explore the inside of her mouth? Would she meet his tongue with her own? He wanted to kiss her, to know again the bright, hot sexuality they'd kindled together. Slowly he reached for her other hand and drew her to him. Her nostrils flared and her eyes widened. The tiny signs of arousal pulled his gut into a tight knot of need and he felt his body begin to respond.

Then, without warning, she withdrew her wrists from the loose clasp in which he held them, backing away until she bumped up against the wall. "I'd better get some rest. Becca's always up early."

Whit allowed her to slide past him. He crossed the floor with her, masking his disappointment. "Why so wary, Susannah?"

Her backbone straightened, and she slowly turned to face him again. "Whit, it's understandable that you think you're attracted to me. I'm carrying your child. But you can't romanticize what's between us. We have a business deal."

He wanted to ask her why she was so sure that the attraction he felt was only a result of the baby. What law said he couldn't feel romantic about her? But when she slipped out of the room and padded softly down the hall, he let her go, standing in the doorway with his fists clenched at his sides to prevent him from hauling her back and kissing her until she couldn't protest any more.

Seven

One week later Susannah gazed morosely out the windows of the morning room where she and Becca were eating breakfast. The sky was leaden and the ocean was full of wild whitecaps frothing and kicking up their heels. The horizon was a single shade of gray with no demarcation between water and sky, and the landscape was brushed with a hazy pall.

The overcast sky matched her mood. Only one week and she was going crazy with boredom. Thank heaven for Becca. If she didn't have the little girl to keep her busy, she'd be stark raving mad. But Becca slept most of the afternoon and went to bed before eight each evening. Susannah had nothing to occupy her during those long hours when she wasn't chasing a child around. Her energy had increased as the nausea decreased; she was starting to feel desperate for something to occupy her time.

She found Whit in the kitchen. She knew he usually came in and washed his hands after his early morning work outside, and today she was waiting for him.

"Hi, baby!" Whit's eager greeting was for Becca. He'd practically ignored Susannah since that night in his office. Although she knew she'd been right to remind him of the reason she was in his life at all, she missed his easy companionship and gentle humor. She even missed the way he used to fuss over her health. As soon as his hands were dry, he swung the little girl up in his arms, holding her high until she squealed. Only then did he turn his gaze to Susannah.

"You two couldn't wait to get out of the house today, huh? Well, I have bad news. I don't think we'd better go down to the beach right now. Tide's up and the waves are big. We're going to get a storm and I don't want to take a chance on getting caught in it."

Susannah's heart sank as she saw the mutinous look on Becca's face.

Whit apparently saw it, too, because he said hastily, "But I have something else we can do if you like."

"Bec-ca do thumteen elth," the tot announced importantly to her mother, as if Susannah hadn't heard Whit.

Whit grinned. Susannah's heart skipped a beat. That boyish, unfeigned expression of pleasure was so rare these days that Susannah could count on the fingers of a single hand the number of times she'd seen it. It was nearly always in connection with Becca.

"I have a collection of seashells," he told Becca. "Would you like to come see them? I'm cleaning some new ones today."

As Becca hollered an enthusiastic "Yeth!" Susannah felt a stab of envy for her two-year-old daughter. It was clearly a one-person invitation. Determined to be gracious, she stood on tiptoe and kissed Becca's cheek. "'Bye, baby. Be a good girl for Whit." The movement brought her face only inches from Whit's, and her pulse quickened at the male scent that assailed her nostrils. She turned away before he could read awareness in her eyes.

"Where are you going?"

"Back to my room."

"If you're not busy, why don't you come with us? I'd like to show you the collection I started."

Suddenly the day seemed brighter. "I'd like that."

The room to which he took them was on the main floor. It was the size of a large garage and only a fraction more appealing. Folding tables stood along the walls, with boxes scattered here and there. Several photographs enlarged, matted and framed, were stacked in a haphazard pile against one wall. Three enormous turtle shells sat on the floor. Stuffed and mounted, a raccoon, a large rabbit and several birds presided over the chaos.

"What is this?" Susannah asked with genuine curiosity.

"The beginning of my Island Habitat room," Whit answered. "Since I was a child, I've collected shells on the beach. Never anything living, of course, but after a hurricane or a storm there are often unusual things left behind. I've saved them all, and last year it occurred to me that I had enough stuff to display. When I got to thinking about it, I decided to collect anything that is indigenous to the island and create a room for the collection. If I find an animal already dead that's in good enough condition, I'm going to have it preserved, as well as the sea life." He gestured at the turtle shells. "These are protected by the federal and state government. I have to report any dead turtles I find. They gave me permission to keep these shells last year after I explained why I'd like to have them."

Susannah slid a finger over a big spiral snail shell protruding from one box. "This looks like quite a job."

"It is. I worked on it this winter, but with the turtles' nesting season and the students arriving soon, I won't be able to do anything in here until at least September. And I doubt I'll get much done next winter with a tiny baby to keep me busy."

Susannah was determined to be as matter-of-fact as he was about their arrangement. "No, you'll have your hands full for the first year or so. Becca's just beginning to display some independence." She glanced fondly at the little girl who was pawing through a box Whit had set on the floor for her.

At the mention of the little girl, an expression of... anxiety almost crossed Whit's features. "I've enjoyed watching the changes in her as she's getting healthier," he said. Then, in an offhand tone, he added, "I hope this baby doesn't have any trouble."

Susannah thought it was a strange thing for him to say. "I had an easy labor with Becca."

"I didn't mean your labor, although I certainly hope it will be an easy one." Whit hesitated. "I don't know of any congenital defects in my family, and I know you don't, either, but I keep reading things about the number of babies born with problems every year, and I can't help wondering if this baby is going to be okay."

She was astounded. "How long have you been worrying about this?"

He looked sheepish. "Since Becca's surgery."

"Why didn't you mention it to me? Or to the doctor?" She reached for a reassuring tone. "Indications are that this baby will be fine. Dr. Bradley would prepare us if he thought there were going to be any complications. Maybe you should call him, though, just to put your mind at ease."

"Maybe." But he seemed happier already.

Before he could dream up anything else to worry about, she hit him with the idea that had occurred to her when she'd been listening to him explain the Island Habitat concept. "Could I help you set up this room?" She'd said it mainly to get him off the topic of birth defects, but she found it appealed to her immensely. The things scattered around the room were fascinating.

Whit seemed taken aback. "You want to help with this?"

Sensing she'd surprised him, Susannah pushed a bit harder. "Oh, yes. I'm going crazy without anything to do!"

"But you're taking care of Becca. You're supposed to be taking it easy, remember?" Whit's jaw set in the way that she was beginning to recognize meant he was going to dig in his heels on something. It only served to make him more attractive.

"Becca sleeps all afternoon. What am I supposed to do then?"

His voice was dry. "Have you tried resting?"

She ignored the amusement dancing in his eyes. "I can't sleep in the afternoon. If I do, then I'm up half the night. I've read until I'm sick of sitting with a book in my hand, and Hilda will cut off my arms if she catches me trying to do any housework other than the dishes. I had to fight just to be allowed to make my own bed!"

Whit laughed. "Yeah. She's kind of funny about that." He looked thoughtfully around the room. "I guess if you promise not to lift any boxes, you could work in here."

Susannah gave him an exasperated glare to compensate for the way her voice had gotten breathless at the warmth in his gaze. "I lift Becca every day."

"And the next time you visit Dr. Bradley, I'm going to find out if you should be doing that."

"You're impossible. Why didn't you warn me you had watchdog blood in your veins?"

"It's for your own good, Mrs. Taylor. Humor me."

Susannah gave an exaggerated sigh. "Tell me what I can do."

Two weeks later Susannah sat back on her heels in front of a newspaper covered with sand dollars. The pretty white shells had dried and she was preparing to arrange them on an empty table when Whit stuck his head into the room.

"I'm going over to the mainland. Want to ride along?" He gave her the lopsided grin that always made her heart leap in response.

Susannah considered for a moment. "I'd love to, but Becca—"

"Hilda said she'd take care of her when she wakes up from her nap. We'll be back before dinner."

Susannah considered the idea as she climbed to her feet. Suddenly she sucked in a quick breath as the room spun around her. "Whoa," she managed. "I'm dizzy."

She clutched frantically at Whit's shirt when he stepped close. His arms came around her, holding her tightly against his lean strength. As the wave of light-headedness receded, she became all too aware of the hard chest beneath the light shirt he wore, the muscled thighs meeting at the junction of widespread male legs, the firm biceps flexing beneath her clenched fingers.

She wasn't wearing maternity clothes yet, and today she'd donned a loose cotton shirt with a pair of her own shorts, leaving the top button and part of the zipper open. When Whit grabbed for her, he'd inadvertently clasped her hip beneath the shirt and now his lean fingers were splayed across her belly. She could feel their heat against her bare skin, and with a rush of embarrassed chagrin, she realized his hand had slipped inside her shorts. Almost as quickly, her starved senses seized on his touch, swelling her breasts until the nipples tightened, sending a rush of liquid warmth to dampen her secret woman's core. Her body's swift sexual reaction stunned her, making a mockery of her attempts to pretend he was just another man, just another means of making ends meet.

She forced herself to meet his gaze.

Adrenaline had rushed through Whit when Susannah sagged against him. Another surge of the same hormone spread through his system, but unlike the first, this one wasn't caused by fear. He hadn't meant to touch her so intimately. But now, holding her against his rapidly hardening body, his fingers spread over the slight bulge where his child grew, all he could think of was the first time he'd taken her to Dr. Bradley's office.

He'd nearly had a heart attack when the obstetrician had matter-of-factly opened Susannah's pants right in front of him. The doctor must have thought he was Mr. Taylor. Susannah's face had turned seven shades of scarlet. Whit had felt his blood pressure coming to a rapid boil as he'd watched the doctor competently knead her tummy, just above peach silk panties that were cut so low he could see the pale gold hair curling out of the lace at the top. Then Dr. Bradley had asked about soreness in her breasts, and Whit's eyes had gone automatically to the topic of discussion, remembering how round and pretty Susannah's breasts had been the night he'd made love to her.

His eyes lit on her breasts now, measuring them against his memories. They seemed bigger to him, fuller under the loose shirts she'd been wearing lately. The skin of her abdomen beneath his hand felt like hot silk, as if she contained a secret source of heat that seared from the inside out. Slowly his thumb moved, brushing back and forth in a tiny, insistent rhythm over the smooth flesh. He lifted his gaze to hers and a charge like a small electrical shock bolted through him when he saw the soft, drowning response on her face. Her lips were parted, the pupils so large that her eyes were nearly black with desire. She watched him with an unfocused gaze, as if she were a mindless automaton waiting for orders from a master.

He couldn't help himself. She felt so good, so right in his arms. Whit moved a fraction closer, sliding the rigid flesh behind his zipper against her softly rounded hipbone as his mouth met hers in open demand. The instant increment of relief at the contact was short-lived and he rocked against her again, and then once more. He was startled and then thrilled when Susannah picked up his movement, shifting her hips in counterpoint to his.

Whit groaned into her mouth. Susannah responded by meeting his tongue with her own, playing a surprisingly bold game of seek-and-retreat. Her unconscious sensuality was driving him wild. Seeking to give her the same mindless degree of need he was experiencing, he slid his hand steadily down over her belly into the thatch of warm curls and below, looking down between their bodies. Susannah jolted once in his arms at the suddenness of his approach, then her body accepted his touch and she relaxed. Taut muscles softened, giving him access to the swollen cleft between her legs. He groaned again when his questing fingers were bathed in the unmistakable moisture of her desire.

Pressing the pad of his middle finger against her, he began a circular motion, pressing and releasing, circling and stroking. Her breath heaved in and out. Glancing up, he saw that her eyes were squeezed tightly closed and her face was a grimace of pleasure too great to be borne. He increased the tempo of his touch, feeling his body clench triumphantly when she cried out and jerked spasmodically in his arms after only a few more short strokes. He was so sensitized that the ungoverned motions of her hips grinding against him sent him over the edge, and while she was still shuddering in his arms, he found his own release in cadence with the unconscious bucking of her body against him.

A long silent moment passed.

Susannah was a limp weight in his arms, her head lowered against his chest. Whit could feel his face burning and knew a wry amusement that he should be the one to blush. Still, he was eaten alive with embarrassment. He hadn't gone off in his pants since he was a teenager—and if he'd done it then he couldn't remember the occasion! What did one say to a woman in these circumstances?

He was suddenly vividly aware that he still had one hand cupped possessively between Susannah's legs; he could feel occasional aftershocks of pleasure quivering through her. His pants felt damp and sticky, unlike his face, which grew hotter with every passing second. Slowly, at a quarter the speed with which he'd delved into her panties, he withdrew his hand. He could feel tension stiffening her body; it mirrored his own.

When his fingers were free, he gently tugged the voluminous shirt back down over the opened waist of her shorts. The action flattened her breasts slightly under the shirt before they sprang back to their normal shape. It hit him that he hadn't so much as touched them, or kissed those rosy crests of which he was constantly dreaming. He felt even more of a creep.

"Susannah, I'm—"

"Please, Whit, can we not talk about this?" Her voice was tight and strained.

Although he recognized embarrassment in her tone, he knew a strange, surprising anger. "Why not?" His voice was harsh but he didn't care. "You turn a man on so fast he humiliates himself in front of you, and you want to *forget about it?*"

Susannah looked astonished. "*You* humiliated yourself? You weren't the one who just—well, you know what happened to me!"

With an incredible tenderness he hadn't known he had in him, he realized she'd been so caught up in the magic they made together that she hadn't even known what she did to him. Smiling crookedly, he released her and stepped back a pace, spreading his arms wide. "You weren't alone. You pack quite a punch, lady."

As her eyes swept over him, comprehension dawned. He could see it in the color that suffused her already pink cheeks, in the hands that flew to cover the mouth that had formed a perfect O. Although he hadn't looked, he knew what she was seeing. The front of his wet pants had to reflect the cataclysmic explosion that had rocked his body minutes before.

Attempting to relieve the tension, Whit said, "This has never happened to me before. Now I know why they say pregnant women are so erotic."

Susannah shook her head sadly. "Not this woman. My ex-husband never touched me when I was pregnant with Becca."

She had to be kidding. Pregnant or not, she was the sexiest woman he'd ever held in his arms. His body certainly knew it. But when he looked into her violet eyes, he saw she was speaking what she thought was the truth. He wanted to take her in his arms again and show her how wrong she was, but he sensed she wouldn't accept it.

Deliberately he framed his next words. "Your ex-husband was a fool."

Again she shook her head. "Steve was many things, but foolish wasn't one of them." The bitterness he'd detected before broke through. "I was the fool. I married him, I got pregnant to try to save a relationship that was already dead. I believed that Becca's problems were all my fault."

As before, he wanted to question her about her marriage. But Axel's voice had them both tensing. "Boat's ready, Whit."

Whit looked over his shoulder at the grizzled caretaker. He'd nearly spun around, but checked the impulse when he remembered the state of his trousers. "Thanks, Axel. We'll be along soon."

When the sound of Axel's footsteps had faded into the distance, Whit returned his gaze to Susannah. "I have to change and then I'll be ready to go."

Susannah turned away. "I'm not going."

In her room, she slipped off her sandals and lay down across the big bed. She'd better enjoy lying on her stomach because soon it wouldn't be comfortable. A sigh whispered across her lips and echoed in the silence. Her mind played the scene in the Island Habitat room over and over again, her body responding to the imagined sensations until she was hot and breathless, an unaccustomed throbbing between her legs a vivid reminder of the conflagration Whit had ignited within her.

How could she have allowed him to touch her like that? How could she have let herself respond so...so wildly?

Finally, though she'd been sure she was too agitated to sleep, her body knew when rest was imperative. As she dozed off, her last thought was of Whit.

Two hours later she arose refreshed, although Whit was still firmly fixed in her head. Wandering over to the window, she scooted her bottom up on the cushioned seat and curled up. Her room was at the back of the house. The big brick home had been built near a hill overlooking the ocean, and she could see the beach where she and Becca often walked with Whit. At high tide now, it was little more than a strip of white over which breakers curled and foamed.

Directly below her was the flagstone patio where she'd sat when she'd been off her feet. Just off the terrace was a verdant strip of lawn that Axel worried over as fiercely as he nursed along the much larger plot of grass at the front of the house. It was to the small green border that Susannah's eyes were drawn.

In the middle of the lawn, within easy distance from the patio, Whit was laboring over a metal frame. Curious, she looked more closely at the contraption. He laboriously attached one crossbar, then another, but it wasn't until he picked up the long, rectangular sheet of flat metal and angled it into place from the top to the ground that she realized she was seeing what Axel and Hilda had been discussing. Whit was putting together a swing set! With a slide attached!

She must've made some movement, because he glanced up at that exact second, zeroing in on the window in which she sat. The sun glinted off his hair, striking copper sparks as he beckoned with one hand. Before she had time to remember the embarrassing scene they'd played out before he went over to the mainland, she nodded back, indicating that she'd come down.

"Want to read me the directions?" His greeting was laconic, but the glance he sent her way brought warmth to her cheeks as she sank onto the grass and picked up the papers he indicated. "I'm one of those people who starts screwing things together first. I look to see how many parts are left after I'm done.''

Susannah ducked her head and stared hard at the writing on the sheets. That hadn't been a "let's pretend nothing happened" look. It had been more of a "want to try it again" one.

"Where are we now?" Her words were meant to refer to the directions, but she was acutely aware of the double entendre as soon as it left her mouth.

Whit only grinned. "Letter Four. Insert Pole C into Something-or-other."

Thank you, God. For whatever reason, he wasn't going to mention what had happened earlier. She was grateful. She didn't want to talk about it. It had simply been one of those unforgivable lapses they'd both have to forget. Dutifully she surveyed the parts spread over the ground around them. "Ah. It goes right up here, into this piece they label B. Looks like you fasten it with these bolts. Here's a nut for the first one."

As he set the piece in place and began to attach it, she asked, "Did you get this today?"

"Uh-huh. I wanted you to help me choose which one would be best for Becca, but..." He shrugged.

Susannah felt horribly guilty. And horribly embarrassed when she remembered the reason she'd decided not to go. "It was thoughtful of you. She's going to love it." Some perverse imp made her add, "Of course, your child will be able to use it in a few years." The mere thought made her heart hurt.

Whit nodded as if he hadn't considered that before. "Yeah. *If* we get it put together. I'm terrible at stuff like this. What next?"

She perused the directions again, pointing out the next step and finding the corresponding parts. "This, I think." As he struggled to attach the piece she indicated, she watched in silence for a moment. "Won't this put you behind with your own work?"

"Probably. But I loathe paperwork and that's all that's on the urgent list right now, so I'm pretending it doesn't exist."

Susannah took a deep breath. "Anything I could help with?"

Whit was silent for so long, she thought perhaps he hadn't heard her, but she knew he must have.

She tried to explain. "I enjoy working on the Island Habitat setup, but there are still a lot of hours in the day. I'm playing with Becca so much that she's forgetting how to entertain herself. I love spending time with her, but I could help you out, if you like."

"You could help me out." The deep tone of his voice made her stomach muscles tense. Was she reading a dual meaning into everything he uttered this afternoon?

She rushed into speech again. "I've done some accounting—I could probably balance your books and statements—and I could do simple correspondence. You could even dictate, if you like."

He threw her a quizzical look. "A lot of my work involves keeping records on the turtles. Charts and graphs, statistics, computer entries, narrative information. If you're really interested, I could show you what I do."

"It sounds challenging." She smiled tentatively. "I've never been idle in my whole life. It's hard for me to sit around here and let Hilda wait on me and you take care of all my needs without me giving something back."

Whit was concentrating on tightening a screw; he didn't look up at her words. "You worked after you were married?"

Susannah's internal alarm system went on when he mentioned her marriage. She never thought of Steve without every nerve in her body tensing. In fury. Smoothing her ruffled feathers, she made her voice calm and even. "Yes. I was a clerical receptionist for a law firm in Atlanta before I came down here."

"You never told me what happened with your marriage." Whit still hadn't made eye contact. She considered telling him it was none of his business, but a surprising desire to share the years of disappointment and loneliness with him caught her flat-footed.

"You know I didn't finish college," she reminded him. "Dumb little co-ed knocked off her feet by handsome successful older man." She mocked herself angrily.

"How much older?"

"Steve was fifteen years older than I was. He had his own import-export business. He was really quite wealthy." She laid the sheets of paper in her lap and looked out across the blue sea. "By the time I'd been married six months, I knew it had been a mistake, but I'd been raised to believe in the sacred institution of marriage. I'd probably still be married to him if he hadn't left."

"He left you?" The amazement in his voice was gratifying.

She smiled briefly at him. "Thanks. That does my ego good." The expression faded into regret. "Yes, he left me. The day Becca was born, to be exact."

Whit's expression held more than mild surprise, and his tone conveyed condemnation. "What a bastard. Why?"

Susannah hesitated. She'd never talked about this to another soul. Not even to Ira, who had been her savior when she'd first come to the coastal area south of Brunswick.

But Whit wasn't about to let her squeak out of an explanation now. "Didn't he want kids?"

She swallowed. This was more painful than she'd expected. Whit dropped his screwdriver in the middle of a twist and came to sit beside her. Reaching for her hand, he cradled it almost protectively between his big, callused palms. "How could any man not want that beautiful little girl?" he asked softly. "If this baby's a girl, I hope she looks just like her big sister."

His words hammered another spike into the aching surface of her heart. As she'd done for days now, she deliber-

ately blanked out all thought of what would occur at the end
of this pregnancy. Her voice quavered and she fiercely
sucked in a steadying breath before she answered him. The
words spewed out now, a catharsis postponed for two long
years. "Oh, it wasn't that Steve didn't want kids. I don't
think he really cared, one way or the other, as long as it
didn't interfere with his social life too much. He was always
going, always dragging me to some party, some event, some
outing that his crowd of hard-drinking, fast-moving friends
were having. It was never something I enjoyed. I married
him with the naive surety that love and companionship
would make all that unnecessary. After two years, I knew
I'd been wrong, but instead of cutting my losses, I decided
a child was the answer."

She mimed knocking herself on the head with the hand
Whit wasn't holding. Before the gesture was complete, he'd
snagged that hand and dragged it down to rest with the
other. "It's a good thing my first pregnancy was easy, because I was alone from day one. When I went into labor,
Steve had to be called at the golf course. He finished his
match first."

Whit's fingers tightened over hers, but she welcomed the
small pain. She concentrated on it, reciting the events surrounding Becca's birth in a flat monotone. "I was alone for
the birth. They knew right away that there was something
drastically wrong. Becca quit breathing and had to be re-
suscitated on the table. Steve came in about an hour later....
That evening, the doctors told us about her heart condition. They grilled us about our family backgrounds, said
this was primarily an inherent disease that genetic counsel-
ing could have prevented. Steve was furious. He told me I
was defective, that he wasn't about to spend every dime he
made taking care of a handicapped kid or paying for years
of medical treatment. He left that night and I never saw him
again."

When she fell silent, Whit prompted her. "But I thought
you told me the problem was in your husband's family."

Susannah laughed, but it was a pathetic parody of humor. "Yeah. The next day I got a visit from Steve's cousin. Rosalie was a kind person. She had no idea Steve had lied to me, and she gave me all the facts and figures he'd omitted. It seems Steve's parents lost two older siblings to this disease before Steve was born, and the entire family knew about the hereditary aspects. Everyone but me.

"I got a letter from Steve that day. He refused to acknowledge Becca as his child. He said if I tried to pursue it, he had witnesses who would swear I'd had an affair. He moved out of our apartment and left. I guess I should have fought back, had blood tests done or something, but I just wanted to forget he existed. I was grateful at the time that he'd left me five thousand dollars. That money kept us going until I could go back to work. Then, after Becca was stabilized, I left Atlanta and moved down here. When Ira hired me, he filed divorce proceedings, and I got my freedom back. I found out later that Steve had had us removed from his insurance policy the day after Becca's birth."

"What about his family? They stood by and let this happen?"

"Steve's parents were dead when we met. He has no siblings and very little close family."

"Does Ira know about all this?" It was a furious demand.

"Yes, he—"

"Why in hell hasn't he nailed that S.O.B. to a wall? Ira has tons of connections. He could make him reimburse you for every penny you've spent in medical expenses. If you'd had financial security, there would never have been a need—" He fell silent, the heaving of his broad chest an indicator of his agitation as the full import of what she was telling him sank in.

Susannah turned her hands in his, squeezing gently. "If Steve wasn't such a monster, you might not be getting your child." She surmised from the stiff set of his shoulders that it had already occurred to him. "Whit, I learned a long time

Eight

The second week of May was the last one he would have before the students arrived. Whit had always looked forward to the change in routine in the past, longing for the day when the first wide turtle track appeared on the beach, looking like a single tractor tire had driven up out of the sea. This year, something was missing. Or perhaps it wasn't that anything was missing as much as he was missing something.

And he knew exactly what it was. Susannah. The only real opportunity to see her now was during the morning walk on the beach with Becca, for which he continued to make time. He'd come to love the little girl dearly, but he sure wished he could spend a moment with her mother without Becca's constant chatter and constraining presence.

Since the day they'd touched each other like lovers, Susannah had been as nervous around him as a lobster who knew it was next in the pot. The easy camaraderie they'd shared was a thing of the past, shredded both by his clumsy attempt at lovemaking and by Susannah's unaccustomed openness about her ex-husband's role in her life.

He almost regretted giving in to impulse that day. Almost. He could've been a gentleman and simply assisted her until the dizziness had passed. But once he'd had her nestled in his arms, once he'd touched the satiny skin below her navel again, once she'd looked up at him as if he were the last sunrise she'd ever see in her life... He liked to think he could've walked away, but deep down he knew he didn't have that kind of strength.

He did know one thing, though. He had to take drastic steps to avoid the attraction between them. It had been bad enough before he'd touched her this time. He'd had three-dimensional memories of how responsive she'd been *that night* to torment him through the dark, lonely night hours. He'd had her scent and the pale glory of her glowing hair to remind him of how good she'd felt beneath him, how she'd wrapped her legs around his waist and accepted the sowing of his seed with pleasure.

He wanted her again. Her body was beginning to change now, his child making its presence known. He'd noticed that she'd begun to wear stretchy shorts under the tops that were getting hard to button. Just yesterday she'd appeared in a voluminous shirt that obviously would give her plenty of room throughout the remainder of her pregnancy. He'd wanted to tease her, but with the new barriers between them, he hadn't felt able to do so.

Now, Hilda informed him breakfast was nearly ready and Whit headed toward the study to pick up the day's schedule. Maybe he'd find Susannah there. She'd gotten into the habit of rising early and doing paperwork for a bit before she went to dress and feed Becca breakfast before their walk on the beach.

The door stood ajar. A good sign. His pulse quickened as he stepped into the room.

Susannah sat at his desk, a big graph of turtle nesting cycles spread in front of her. The tip of her pink tongue was caught between her teeth as she painstakingly added points to the graph, then connected them with a ruler. He noted with amusement and a bit of pride that she was wearing another one of the big shirts today. Her body was changing noticeably. The early morning sun filtered through the window, glancing off her bright hair in a halo of pale light. Even the fierce golden rays couldn't add gold to the gleaming silver mass of curls.

"You work too hard." He hadn't meant to startle her, but she jerked her head up and the pencil between her fingers clattered to the desk.

She fixed him with an accusing stare. "I didn't hear you come in."

Whit grinned, unable to hide the pleasure he felt at simply sharing the same air with her. "You were so immersed in those figures I could've driven the Jeep through here without you noticing."

"Now let's not exaggerate." But she was smiling. "Is it time for Becca to get up already?"

"'Fraid so. If you want to take a walk this morning."

"*If?* Since when was this an option?"

Whit laughed. "You're right. Becca thinks it's a permanent part of my routine."

He'd been glad to see how relaxed she appeared to be this morning. The usual cautious mask hadn't yet fallen into place, but at his words, she sobered. "Whit, you don't have to do this now that your schedule's getting busier. Becca and I can entertain ourselves."

Whit considered her motives. She hadn't said she didn't like his company. She'd sounded genuinely concerned that they were cutting into his workday. "Are you kidding?" He deliberately kept his reply light. "These walks are the highlight of my day. Would you deprive me of the chance to educate your daughter about the ecological environs of the beach?"

Susannah laughed. The sound warmed the supremely masculine study with a deliciously feminine atmosphere.

"When you put it that way, I could hardly refuse." She tidied the desk top, then rose and walked across the room to where he was still leaning in the doorway. "I'll get Becca. We'll meet you in the dining room in ten minutes." When she moved past him, her belly brushed against his hip. The warmth of her flesh knifed into him, settling at a point midway between his hipbones. How could a pregnant woman be so sexy? He stayed where he was long after she'd slipped past him, holding up the door frame with one broad shoulder. He felt keen excitement, anticipation, the same way he felt every morning before these moments he spent in Susannah's company. He also felt apprehension.

He knew what he was feeling. If he were smart, he'd get her out of his house this weekend. She was clearly feeling better, and he didn't doubt she could manage in her own home now. He couldn't afford to fall in love with Susannah Taylor. She was only a short-term visitor on Turtle Island. He knew very well how women felt about his chosen home. She'd be just as horrified as the rest if he were to ask her to make her home here.

Besides, he couldn't be in love with her. The only reason she appealed so strongly to him was because of the circumstances, just as she'd said. Anyone could be forgiven for thinking he was in love with the mother of his child...but what if he asked her to stay on the island and she threw his offer back in his face? He'd sworn he'd never let rejection slap him in the face again.

Forty minutes later he stopped on a steep section of path and offered a hand to Susannah. The small gesture had become a ritual since Whit had realized how very cautiously she navigated the treacherous path that led from the house to the beach. He'd apologized profusely and extracted a promise from her to ask for help anyplace in which she felt unsure. By now, he knew when to offer assistance before she requested it.

On his shoulders, Becca wriggled and demanded, "Go, Whit!"

"Wait a minute," he responded, squeezing her tiny knee hard enough to make her scream and giggle. "I'm helping Mommy."

When they reached the beach a few moments later, he set Becca down in the sand, watching in amusement as she made a beeline for the waves. Although she invariably walked right at the water's edge, Whit knew that Becca never did more than get her big toe wet. Consequently today he stayed by Susannah's side, walking idly through the warming sand in the same direction as the inquisitive toddler.

"Ouch!" Her sudden exclamation stopped them both. "I stepped on a sharp piece of shell, I think." Holding onto Whit's arm for balance, Susannah examined the bottom of her foot.

"Did it break the skin?"

"No." She shook her head. "But it stung for a minute." Dropping his arm, she resumed walking.

"I told you you should wear shoes." His voice was the faintest bit smug.

"And now you'll never let me forget it," Susannah said dryly. "I don't care. I enjoy walking in the sand in bare feet. A few cuts are a small price to pay."

Whit laughed. "I'll wind up carrying you if the going gets too tough." Unable to resist, he reached over and linked her fingers through his, swinging their clasped hands between them as they walked. When she didn't pull away, he was elated.

They walked on for several hundred yards, following Becca's meanderings as she examined a starfish that had washed up at high tide and discovered numerous shells that she placed in the small bucket she was carrying. Whit let go of Susannah's hand and sprinted over to head off Becca when she found a dead sand shark rolling over and over in the surf. He took time to explain that even when an animal looks dead, it could still be alive and that she should never touch it.

Susannah stood behind him, and when he deemed it time to turn around and head back, she willingly allowed him to take her hand again.

"Whit hold Mommy's han'!" He'd noticed how much Becca's language had improved since he'd met her five months ago. "Whit hold Becca's han', too."

With a smile, he took her tiny palm in his free one and they all strolled back the way they'd come. Flanked by the two who were rapidly assuming an enormous importance in his life, Whit decided he couldn't be more content if he were in heaven. Well, maybe the icing on the cake would be to have Susannah in his bed every night.

What would he do when they were no longer here to share his days? A huge emptiness yawned, and no matter how often he told himself his own child would fill all the lonely minutes, a small part of him knew nothing could replace Susannah and her daughter.

Not even his own child.

As they began to walk across the lawn, he murmured, "We have company."

Company? Susannah glanced up, not sure she'd heard him right. Since when did they get visitors on the island? The familiar figure standing on the terrace made her smile in spontaneous delight. "Ira!"

"Hello, there." The silver-haired lawyer examined Susannah openly as she crossed the flagstones toward him. She doubted he'd missed the casual way Whit had been holding her hand, though he didn't comment. Instead he said, "You're certainly looking better than you did the last time I saw you."

"I'm feeling better, too," she assured him. "I could probably come back to work."

"No, you couldn't." Whit set Becca down and she ran off toward the kitchen door. "We're just getting into the busy season and you promised to help me with the paperwork. Besides, the doctor wants you to take it easy, remember?"

He looked hard at Ira. "You told me you could get along without her until after the baby came."

Ira held up both hands, laughing. "And I can. Not easily, I admit, but I can. Calm down, Whit. I didn't come to take her back. I need your signature on a few forms to process the inheritance after the stipulations of the will are met, and I thought I'd take the opportunity to see how Susannah was doing."

Susannah smiled, looking fondly at Ira. "I'm just fine. Don't let me keep you from a vital discussion."

"Oh, this isn't vital." Ira gestured at the glass table beneath a yellow and white striped umbrella. "In fact, we can do this right here, Whit. Then, after the baby's born, you'll only have to sign one more document, attesting that the child is indeed your rightful heir, before the bulk of the estate is legally back in your hands."

Susannah stood, riveted in place by the unexpected words. What did Ira mean? Why was her baby important to Whit's estate?

"Sounds good to me," Whit responded. The two men had moved to the table and Ira was pointing out places that needed Whit's signature. "I'll be glad when this ordeal is finally over. I still don't understand why Granddad tied my inheritance up with a ridiculous condition like this. I told him a hundred times I wouldn't marry just to provide him with grandchildren. After what happened with Marguerite, I thought he understood how serious I was."

Their voices faded away as Susannah contemplated the ugly meaning of Whit's last words. She barely noticed when Ira kissed her cheek and said goodbye. In a detached way, she saw him cross to the Jeep Axel must've loaned him. Apparently he wasn't used to driving a clutch, because the vehicle jerked into gear across the lawn in a great burst of speed, followed by several rapid tire-squealing applications of the brakes that nearly threw Ira out over the dash.

As Ira disappeared into the trees, Whit stretched his arms above his head; his spontaneous laughter rolled out over the rich green of his handyman's beloved lawn.

Susannah didn't laugh with him. Deliberately she turned away, heading for the table where a tray of drinks sat, droplets of moisture forming from the contrast between the heat of the day and the icy liquid inside the glasses. Picking one up, she rolled its welcome coolness back and forth over her forehead.

Part of her wanted to scream, "I want an explanation and I want it now!" But another part, the part that always won out when she experienced an internal temper upheaval such as she was wrestling now, said, "Would you like to tell me why Ira is concerned about this baby being your 'rightful heir'?"

The grin he'd been wearing faded to a wary smile as her strained tone penetrated his amusement. Whit reached a hand out, intending to offer her a seat, but she backed away from him. Clearly shocked, he simply stared at her for a moment.

"Am I to understand that this child is a means to a monetary goal for you?" Her voice started out level, but was close to strident by the time she'd finished.

Whit opened his mouth defensively. He closed it again on a sigh. In her violet eyes he read fury and more than a little hurt as she interpreted his damning silence.

Before he could decide how to phrase his answer, Susannah was speaking again. Each word was as cool and brittle as an icicle. "When Ira approached me about your situation, I was led to believe that you wanted a baby because you wanted to be a father. Unless I'm mistaken, you want a baby primarily because you need an heir. Am I correct?"

"Partially," Whit conceded. "But it's not that simple—"

"Then explain it to me in terms I can understand, Whit. *I want to know exactly why you decided to hire a surro-*

gate—'' Susannah stopped abruptly, putting a hand to her mouth.

She'd been shouting. Whit had never heard her raise her voice before today. From the expression on her face, she'd surprised even herself. A ripple of foreboding ran through him.

"Let's sit down." He pulled one of the wrought-iron chairs over and brushed imaginary specks of dust off its cushioned surface before offering it to her. When she sat, he retrieved a chair for himself and settled it at an angle from hers so that he could easily see her face.

Susannah picked up a glass of lemonade and sipped. Her silence was a demand for an explanation in itself.

"My grandfather raised me," Whit began. "He was delighted with the turtle program I began here on the island after I finished school, and his fondest wish was that I would raise my children to follow in my footsteps. Unfortunately I didn't produce any children for him to dote over. He was always after me about settling down, but I never realized exactly how much it meant to him.

"When he died last October, Ira handled his estate. When Ira read the terms of the will, I was in a state of shock for more than a month. I had been reared with the understanding that I would inherit the island someday. The Montgomery family hasn't flourished in recent times and I'm the only direct heir."

He stopped and took a sip of lemonade. Susannah didn't say a word, nor did she look at him. Instead she swirled her drink around and around in its glass, concentrating on the motion with almost fanatical attention. Her lovely face was carefully composed and he couldn't imagine what she was thinking. The anxiety he was feeling coalesced into a knot of tension in the pit of his stomach. He didn't know what else to do but go on.

"My grandfather willed everything to me, as I had expected. There was one stipulation. I have to produce a biological heir within one year from the date the will was read to retain my inheritance. Otherwise, the entire estate will be liquidated.''

Susannah looked blank. ''You'd still get the money, wouldn't you?''

''It's not the money!'' Whit's voice was sharper than he'd intended. He took a deep breath and tried to make her understand. ''That's not strictly true. It *is* the money, but not because I want to live like a king. Look around us, Susannah.'' He gestured with one big hand. ''Do I squander my money on an opulent life-style?''

''Opulent, no, but you certainly don't worry about the cost if you see something you want.''

Whit was getting angry. She was going to condemn him without a trial. ''My grandfather was a terrific judge of human nature. He knew my life's work with the turtles is the only thing that matters to me. Within hours of the reading of the will, there were real estate appraisers over here estimating how much this place will be worth on the block. If the island is sold, it will be developed. Sea turtles all over the world are losing the few nesting beaches they have left. If this island is developed, the turtles will have to find another place to nest. There are next to none. In addition, the turtles return to the same beaches to nest. They often make their new nest mere yards from the last one they laid two seasons ago! If this nesting ground is disturbed, who knows how many turtles will be lost? Don't you see? I can't let this land be sold. It could be a fatal blow to an already endangered species.''

''What about asking for help from the government?''

He'd known Susannah wouldn't simply swallow his arguments. In some obscure way, her quick thinking pleased him even as his agitation grew. ''Do you think I haven't tried that? They're so overextended they could only wish me luck. I called every source I could think of. Nobody can assure me they'd outbid the speculators. Prime coastal real estate like this goes for a mint. But if I could have been sure the land would be purchased by an environmental group that would

let me continue my work, I'd have done it in a heartbeat."
He snapped his fingers to emphasize his point. "I don't care
how many millions there are in my inheritance. If I wanted
the money, I'd probably be smart to let it go to the highest
bidder. But I want to save the land for the turtles and this
seems to be the only way I can do it."

When he finished, Susannah was still swirling her drink.
"Well?"

"Well, what?" She wasn't giving an inch.

"Do you understand why I had to do it?"

She nodded slowly. "Yes, Whit, I do understand. I ap-
plaud you for trying to save a species. But I have some grave
concerns about your motivation for wanting this child. I
need to think about whether I want to challenge the surrogate contract."

Whit sucked in a breath. The fist in his stomach closed
and squeezed painfully. "Challenge the contract?"

Susannah nodded again. Her eyes were a smoky violet,
darkened with emotion, as they held his. "I'm not sure you
want this baby for its own sake. Would you have considered adding a child to your life this way without that will
telling you you had to produce offspring?"

"No." He didn't even hesitate. "I equated children with
love and marriage. I'd resigned myself to having neither.
Can you truly imagine a woman content to live out here?"
He didn't give her a chance to reply. "I'll be honest with
you. I would never have chosen this without pressure, but
it's been an exciting idea. I'm looking forward to being a
father."

Susannah turned her head and looked out at the sea. Whit
studied the pure, clean lines of her profile: the high forehead, the long, sweeping lashes, the slim, straight nose. The
delicate jawline hardly looked pugnacious. If he hadn't
heard her words himself, he'd never have believed she could
sound so firm.

So threatening. Panic rose. She wouldn't—*couldn't*—take
his child away. Would she? Could she?

He surged to his feet. "I want this baby, Susannah, and not because of how it figures in any will." She gave no sign that she'd heard him. Knowing that she wouldn't listen now, he began to walk away.

"Whit?"

Her quiet voice stopped him in his tracks, but he didn't turn around. "What?"

"Who was Marguerite?"

He snorted. "Someone I thought I loved a long time ago."

"Why didn't you marry her?"

"She was no more interested in living out here than my mother was." His tone was flat. "Unlike my father, I had the good sense to recognize it before I put the ring on her finger."

An hour later Whit stalked along the beach, his feelings heaving and rolling inside him like the sea in a hurricane. In his worst nightmares, the one thing he had never considered was that Susannah would try to back out of the surrogate contract. Although Ira had tried to dissuade him from this method of gaining a child, citing gloomy statistics of record numbers of cases in which the mother changed her mind, Whit had pursued it anyhow. And after he'd met Susannah, she'd impressed him as someone who set great store by her personal code of honor. He'd felt perfectly comfortable with their arrangement, confident that the one thing he'd never have to worry about was a change of heart on Susannah's part.

He'd been incredibly wrong, stupidly wrong. Even though he'd seen the longing on her face every time the baby was mentioned, he'd felt so secure in her word that he hadn't worried. What a dope. He'd been fantasizing about asking her to stay on the island and be a mother to his child as well as her own. He'd even been thinking of marrying her. He'd been beginning to think maybe, just maybe, she was going to prove him wrong about women and be the one who could adjust to, even enjoy, life on Turtle Island. How many times did he have to be hit over the head before he realized that he just wasn't meant to have a woman in his life?

Two weeks had passed since the students had arrived on Turtle Island. Susannah awoke before dawn one morning and dressed quickly in the dim light.

Quietly she crossed the floor and knocked hesitantly at the door connected to Whit's room. Perhaps he was already up and gone. She knocked again, and when there was no response, she told herself she'd missed him. But some small impulse made her fingers wrap around the cool brass of the knob, made her twist it to the right, so gently that the tiny click of the latch giving way was nearly soundless. Slowly she pressed against the rich, dark wood. The door swung inward on well-oiled hinges.

Whit's room was lighter than hers, the heavy draperies open even at night to the sight of the island he loved so much. Susannah stood in the doorway, her gaze riveted to the big bed that filled the space between the two long windows. Whit lay on the bed, unmoving.

Did he always sleep without covers?

He lay face down, arms flung wide. The covers were trailing off the foot of the bed just as they'd been the night he'd held her. He wore not a stitch of clothing and his skin gleamed pearly pale where the sun was prevented from turning his flesh to teak. His dark head was buried underneath a pillow. Her gaze traveled down his thick neck, over the wide shoulders and powerful arms, arms she knew could flip a three-hundred-pound turtle. Her visual exploration lingered for a moment on a trim waist before exploring sculpted buttocks untouched by the sun's kiss and long, sinewed legs browned to a crisp toast.

Her feet carried her forward without a conscious command from her brain. Closer now, the curling hairs on his forearms and legs and those peeping from under his arms gave texture to the smooth tones of skin.

She wanted to touch him, to reach out and trail her fingertips over every inch of his firmly fleshed frame, to sink
down beside his big, naked body and pull him over her. She
knew a fierce longing to have him inside her, filling her with
the ultimate expression of his potent masculinity.

But she didn't dare. Turning, she began to retreat from
the room on shaking legs when his voice stopped her.

"Susannah? What's wrong?"

Behind her, she could hear the rustle of fabric sliding over
flesh as the shorts on the floor disappeared from her pe-
ripheral vision. "Nothing's wrong. I wanted to tell you
something."

"About what? The baby?"

"Yes."

"What?" Alarm flared in his tone. He moved into her
line of vision and laid his hands on her shoulders.

"Don't panic." She tried a smile. "It's only... the baby's getting stronger every day and I think you could feel
him kicking now. If you want to."

Whit stared at her. Slowly his hands slid from her shoulders. His gaze was suddenly remote and cool. "Have you
decided I'm fit to be a father, then?"

Susannah understood immediately. "I haven't made any
decision yet about the contract. But I don't see any reason
to deprive you of the baby's development in the mean-
time."

The room was silent while he weighed her words. She
could almost read the struggle going on in his head. He eyed
her belly with a mixture of longing and mistrust. The longing won. "He's kicking?"

She took one of his hands and flattened it over the shirt
covering her distended abdomen. The heat of him distracted her, as always, and she paused momentarily. "Well,
he's stretching or something. I'm not sure if it's a kick."

Whit nodded silently as he relaxed visibly, his eyes focused on the mound under his hand.

The baby moved again.

"Did you feel that?" Susannah demanded.

"Yeah!" Whit's tone was awed, reverential. "What's it feel like to you?"

"It's hard to describe." She thought for a moment. "It doesn't hurt. When I get closer to term, it might get more uncomfortable as he gets bigger and more cramped. But right now—" She spread her hands helplessly. "It's more an awareness that I'm never alone. It almost tickles sometimes when he squirms around. The thuds you feel aren't painful."

"You keep saying 'he,'" Whit accused. "Are you and that doctor in cahoots?" He moved his hand as he spoke, brushing aside her loose top and edging down the stretchy fabric panel at the front of her shorts until his hand was resting against her bare skin.

His touch was too much. Flames licked at the edges of her resistance to his charm; she could feel her self-control curling and cracking in the heat of his magnetism. Torn between exasperation and affection, Susannah stared down at the top of his black head as he bent over her abdomen. The hair grew in a thick wave that swirled out in a perfect circle from the crown of his head. He cocked his head and looked into her face and she realized he was waiting for a response.

She efficiently moved the offending fabric more fully out of the way, murmuring, "Be my guest."

He had the grace to look shamefaced, but there was a twinkle in the navy eyes. "Sorry. I wanted to be right next to him, if it really is a *him*."

At his reminder that she hadn't answered his question, she said, "Don't hold your breath. I don't have any inside information. I called Becca 'him' for nine months, so you can see how reliable I am."

Whit dropped his head again. "I don't care if it's a girl." Bending even further over her swollen belly, he said, "Do you hear me? This is your daddy speaking. I don't care if you're a boy or a girl, if you're blond or dark-haired, if you have blue eyes or violet. I just can't wait for you to get here so I can hold you." He laughed in delight when another kick punched against the resilient flesh beneath his hand. "Did you feel that? He knows me!"

"I felt it." Susannah's tone was dry. She knew a surprising delight that she was able to give him this joy. Mixed with it was the ever-present pain, like a sore tooth exposed to sugar, that descended every time she remembered that as far as this child was concerned, she was merely a vessel, a handy incubator regulating favorable growth conditions until the baby was ready to live on its own. With its father.

"I've been reading some research about bonding. There's evidence that an infant who hears its father's voice for significant quantities of time in utero responds more positively to the father than an infant who hasn't heard its father's voice or has heard it sporadically." Whit paused, looking at her expectantly.

Susannah smiled. Despite what she was feeling, she couldn't be harsh or cold to him. He was so endearing when he got on his horse and rode full-tilt into a lecture. "Do I hear a question in there?" She placed her hand atop his and slid it to one side as another little limb made itself known.

"Yeah, I guess you do. I'd like to make time every day to do this. Not necessarily to touch him—you—" he amended as if he'd just realized how intimate their position was "—but to talk to the baby." Whit followed the movement of their hands with his gaze, carefully avoiding her eyes.

"We can do that. And I don't mind you touching me." Susannah kept her voice composed, trying not to show the elation that shot through her, banishing her unsavory thoughts. Spend time alone with Whit every day! Her common sense told her it wasn't a smart move, that it could only lead to heartache in September. Her heart was doing a tap dance around the room, wildly imagining those callused fingers touching her skin tenderly as if he cared about her.

She looked down at the spot where his big hand showed beneath her much smaller one, widespread fingers flat against her pale skin. *Face it,* she told herself. *You want him*

*to love you. You want him to beg you to marry him and live
on this lonely island for the rest of your life, cut off from
everything you've ever considered important.*

To her astonishment, she realized that the conveniences
she'd considered so vital mere weeks ago were now less than
nothing compared to what was truly important to her. If
Whit wanted her, she'd say yes so fast he'd wonder what hit
him.

Beneath her fingers, Whit's hand began to stroke a small
circle. Her body immediately recognized the sensual nature
of his touch and her breathing changed, growing fast and
shallow as he lifted his gaze to meet hers. There was a fierce,
hot look there that she'd seen before.

"Susannah...I enjoy touching you." Whit's voice was
husky. "Will you—"

A brisk knock at the door was followed so quickly by the
panel swinging open that Hilda was in the bedroom before
she realized Whit wasn't alone. "You'd better be on your
feet if you..." Her voice trailed into a shocked silence,
echoing the expression on her face as she took in the scene.

Susannah froze in embarrassment. She had an all-too-
vivid picture of how they must look, her clothes awry, Whit
wearing only a pair of shorts, his hand held fast by her own
on a decidedly intimate portion of her anatomy. Regaining
her senses, she would've jerked away, but Whit's grip was
suddenly rock-hard and inflexible, holding her without any
discernible effort.

"Thanks," he said to Hilda. His voice was as casual as if
the scene before her were a daily occurrence already. "We'll
be down to breakfast in a minute."

Hilda's steel-wool head gave one curt bob. She turned and
left the room quickly.

Whit stirred. He looked regretful as he removed his hand
from her belly and pulled the fabric of her shorts and shirt
back into place.

Nine

———

Several days later Susannah laid down her dishcloth and removed the big apron that had protected her clothes. Hilda had most of the after-dinner cleanup completed and Susannah knew that her help would no longer be tolerated.

A glance out the window showed a beautiful sunset beginning to tinge the sky. "Want to take a walk?" she asked Becca.

"No, Mommy. Becca 'tay wif Hilda. Make cookies."

Susannah stared at her daughter in astonishment. Reaching out a hand, she laid it on the child's brow. "Maybe she's sick," she said to Hilda. "That's the first time she's ever refused an offer to go outside."

Hilda threw her a distinctly smug smile. She crooked one freckled arm around the child and gave her a brief hug. "No kid in their right mind would choose a walk over a batch of cookies. You go on. I'll take care of her for a while."

"Whit's on the oceanside beach, down a mile or so," Axel told her. "If you're going down there, you can save me a trip. Take the stat sheet from the clipboard in the hall."

Susannah nodded. Slipping out the back door with the form in one hand, she hefted one of the sturdy walking sticks Whit liked her to use when she walked alone. She started down the path to the beach, keeping an eye out for snakes.

When she reached the steep slope that overlooked the beach, she forgot about anything but picking her way carefully down the incline. Maybe this hadn't been such a good idea. She'd probably have to ask for assistance back to the house since it would surely be dusk by then.

She walked briskly along the beach right at the edge of the waves, carrying her sandals. The sand was firm and cool beneath her bare soles and the froth of white foam that brushed her toes occasionally was a whisper of iced delight. Far down the beach she caught sight of a solitary stick figure. She knew from the dinner conversations she'd heard that Whit stationed his volunteers every half mile or so. They were responsible for observing any turtle that came in from the sea to nest and marking the location of the nest after the female crawled back into the ocean.

She quickened her pace. Would this be Whit? It was. Although he was walking slowly down the beach away from her, the broad-shouldered figure was unmistakable.

"Whit!"

His head came up. He spun around. After a moment of hesitation, he began to stride rapidly back the way he'd come. As he neared her, she could see his face, set in unsmiling lines.

"What are you doing down here?"

Not exactly the greeting she'd hoped for. "Looking for you," she said neutrally.

"Alone?"

When she nodded, his face drew into a frown. "You mean you came down the path from the house *alone?*"

"Yes." She didn't like feeling defensive. "But I had a walking stick. I was careful."

"Susannah, 'careful' isn't a guarantee around here. If you fell, you could be there all night until someone found you." He drew a breath, obviously prepared to go on with his lecture.

Susannah stepped into the breach. "I won't be confined to the house like a tropical plant. Normally, I wouldn't have chosen this for an evening stroll without someone to help me up and down the slope, but Axel asked me to bring you these forms."

As she'd hoped, he was diverted. Although his eyes narrowed when she dug in her heels, he let it pass. "Thanks." He folded the form and stuffed it into his pocket. Taking her elbow, he guided her into a leisurely stroll in the direction she had come. When he dropped her arm, the air temperature around her seemed to drop ten notches. "These studies have really been helpful. We're learning more about turtles every day. I hope we can use that knowledge to educate the world to the need to protect them."

Susannah was touched, as always, by the fervor in his voice when he mentioned his work. "I hope you're successful."

"Yeah. Me, too. Otherwise we're going to be losing another species in a few years."

Subdued by his blunt comment, Susannah walked beside him in silence for a while. His words ran around and around in her head and she finally asked, "Are you really concerned about the turtles becoming extinct?"

Whit snorted. "I've gone beyond 'concerned.' Now I'm more like 'resigned.' Unless we can educate the public a lot faster than we have to date, these turtles don't have a chance. And I'm not just talking about loggerheads. I'm talking about all the sea turtles. *Kemp's* ridley is so close to extinction now that there's little hope it can be saved."

"But you think you can make a difference with the loggerheads?"

"I hope so. Loggerheads are in far better shape than most of the others right now. There are several loggerhead projects on the other islands. Little Cumberland has the oldest one in existence. If we can educate people to the plight of the turtles, make them aware of the ecological effects of developing every ounce of coastline, these turtles just might make it. Even then, their survival is going to depend on significant changes in the fishing industry and pollution control in the oceans."

He was in an expansive mood, despite the sober topic. Wanting to keep him talking, she asked, "What kind of changes?"

"Legislation mandating Turtle Excluder Devices is already in effect, but heavy penalties for refusing to use them aren't always imposed. Better enforcement of the endangered species act would help. It's hard to make these people understand that the way they've done things for generations simply has to change, especially when they view turtles as nothing more than stupid critters who rip up their nets."

"When you teach your summer students about sea turtles, you're making a start, though. What do your volunteers do besides patrol the beaches?"

Whit gestured with his hands. "Oh, lots of things. One group each night is on 'hatchery duty.'"

"What's that mean?"

"Loggerheads are notoriously careless about nesting. Some species of sea turtles are quite finicky about the location of their nests, but loggerheads usually only crawl up the beach until they pass the high-tide mark before digging their nests. Excessively high water and predators can destroy the nests before the hatchlings are ready to come out. So we move the eggs to a safer location after the female turtle returns to the sea. When we find a nest, we mark it. Then a crew comes along and digs up the eggs. They take them to the hatchery and rebury them. When the baby turtles hatch, we return them to the sea."

"What a good idea! I bet that saves a lot of turtles."

"More than you know. If we don't get to the nests pretty quickly, ghost crabs and raccoons get in them and kill a lot of the incubating hatchlings. We're very lucky here on Turtle Island not to have feral hogs. Wild pigs love turtle eggs and they're as bad or worse than the 'coons on some of the other islands. Another benefit to moving the eggs is that when we escort the hatchlings down to the sea, the ghost crabs can't pick off nearly as many as they do under normal circumstances." He laughed, but it was a sound of frustration rather than humor. "They're bold little rascals."

Susannah risked a glance at Whit. She loved the way his face lit up when he was talking about the turtles. One of the things that made him so attractive to her was his commitment to his cause.

Intercepting her gaze, his own eyes grew intense. Releasing her elbow, he slid his palm up across her shoulder blades until it rested comfortably on her opposite shoulder. The action drew her against his side, sliding her hip over his with every step she took. She shivered beneath his arm, unable to control the purely sexual reaction that his touch provoked.

Immediately his hold tightened. "Are you cold? I don't want you getting sick." He swung her around to face him, placing both arms around her in a protective gesture.

Cold? She wasn't cold—far from it! His earthy masculine scent surrounded her, his hard fingers heated her skin. It wasn't fair, she thought. No other man in the whole world had this effect on her body. No man made her tremble with only his presence at her side. No man made her long to press her lips against the hair-roughened hollow at the base of his throat.

She lifted her head almost desperately. "Whit..."

He wasn't looking at her eyes. His dark gaze was fastened on her lips. "Susannah..." he mocked softly. Slowly he lifted a finger and traced the curve of her upper lip.

"What?" Her mouth moved against his finger when she spoke. There wasn't enough oxygen in the air—desperately she gasped in a breath.

He smiled down at her. "Isn't that my line?"

"Um, I don't know."

A chuckle worked its way up from his wide chest. "What *do* you know?"

Her mind was blank. Like a stone tablet untouched by a stylus. Grasping at anything that popped into her head, she said, "Something smells bad." Sanity trickled back. "*Really* bad."

"Yeah. Dead fish, probably." Whit frowned reluctantly. "Would you like to come with me where there's no smell?"

What was he asking? Did he want what she thought he wanted? What she wanted more than anything she could imagine? "I can't stay. It's almost Becca's bedtime."

"Hilda can put her to bed. Come with me." He released one shoulder and placed his other arm around her back, holding her snugly against his hip. "I want to show you— Dammit!"

Susannah's head flew up in surprise. The expletive was uncharacteristic. Whit rarely swore.

He released her completely and stepped around her down the sloping beach toward the ocean. Following, she saw what had caused his outburst. The turtle was huge. Its brownish shell moved slightly with each wash of the incoming tide, yellow limbs and scaly head protruding from the enormous bony plate. It was clearly dead.

Susannah sucked in a sympathetic breath. She nearly gagged. As the turtle washed closer, the smell was indescribable. Year-old eggs, a dead skunk, rotting tuna...all mixed together, they didn't come even close. Against her every effort, the gorge rose to choke her. She whirled and ran a safe distance up the sand. Dropping to her knees, she abandoned her walking stick and bent her head, taking several deep breaths until the smell of the putrefying reptile left her nostrils.

"You okay?" Whit was standing nearly on top of the dead beast. She nodded, briefly amazed that the odor didn't seem to bother him. Apparently sure that she was all right, he gave his complete attention to the animal washing in with the tide, occasionally poking it with a foot.

Susannah studied the dead loggerhead. She'd come down to the beach and watched the nesting several times, but she'd never seen a dead loggerhead before. The reptiles were always bigger than she'd expected, even though Whit had told her most of them weighed between two and three hundred pounds. This one's shell, which she knew was called a carapace, was a reddish brown. It wasn't round like the box turtles she'd grown up with, but somewhat elongated, with the pointier section in the back. The turtle's four flippers were a dirty yellow. Looking more closely, she realized that this particular turtle had only three flippers. One of the back ones had been torn off—fairly recently by the looks of it. She wondered if that was what had killed it.

At last Whit straightened and came sprinting up the beach to where she waited. His face was a grim mask.

"Is it one of yours?" Susannah could hardly bear to ask the question.

When he nodded wordlessly, she put her hand on his arm. "I'm sorry."

Again he only nodded and she saw that he was fighting tears. Throwing his head back, hands on his hips, he studied the sky for a long minute. Diamond drops of moisture sparkled at the corners of his eyes. Finally he spoke.

"Big Mama. That's what we called her. She's been coming in to nest since I first started tagging turtles here when I was seventeen.... She was the first turtle I ever tagged." He shook his head slightly. "She put up one hell of a fight when I tried to turn her over, too. I learned real quick how *not* to approach a loggerhead. She comes in faithfully every other year, nesting three or four times a season."

"Did a shark get her?"

"The missing flipper on her back left side was probably a shark's meal after she died, but no, I don't think a shark got her. It's darn near impossible for a shark to kill a full-grown loggerhead unless it cracks the carapace. Her shell doesn't have so much as a tooth mark on it."

"What did she die of?" Susannah couldn't imagine an animal less likely to be victimized by other denizens of the ocean.

Whit's head snapped down fiercely. His tone was just as fierce and his eyes shot blue flame. "You want to know what killed her? You're looking at him, Susannah." He stabbed a finger into his own chest, then into hers. "Man. Not me, not you, but other members of our species. I'd bet my life that turtle drowned in a shrimper's net. We're one of the only things in that whole damned big watery world out there that a mature sea turtle has to fear."

He gestured wildly toward the rosy horizon. "Men. Men with fishnets who trawl so long that any turtles caught in their nets drown before they bother to bring them up. Men who refuse to use TEDs because they're too much trouble. Men who are so busy catching shrimp to feed the growing market for fresh seafood that they couldn't care less whether they kill a few turtles."

Wearily he scrubbed a hand down his face. Both shoulders sagged in defeat. "Who am I kidding? Even if I can keep this island from being developed, there aren't going to be any turtles to come back here one of these days. Some year I'll wait in vain for a single turtle to come in."

"That can't be true! Surely there are things you can do to stop the shrimpers from killing them." Feeling helpless, she looked back down the sand at where the rotting turtle lay, lapped by little wavelets. She'd never seen Whit question himself before. She'd begun to doubt that he ever felt unsure, insecure, unable to bend the world to his making. When Becca had been ill, she hadn't felt a moment's fear after he'd come. He'd been so positive everything would be all right that he'd made her believe it, too.

Now all her perceptions had changed. He needed her. For the first time since she'd known him, she had something to give him, even if it were only a gift of temporary strength.

Impulsively she stepped forward and took his face between her hands. "This island is your child's heritage. *Our* child's heritage. You've committed your life to saving one of God's creatures from extinction, and you've made me care about it, too. *Don't you dare give up now, Whit Montgomery!*"

When he reached up and circled her wrists with his own big hands, she knew a sense of rightness. His body brushed lightly against hers. The sensation quickened her heartbeat and sent arrows of need pulsing down to the junction of her legs. When his dark head slowly lowered, she held her breath, wanting his kiss with every fiber of her heart and mind.

He pulled her closer and lowered his head to find her mouth, his tongue seeking hers without hesitation. Susannah knew a sense of completeness. Their mouths meshed with the surety of familiar lovers, and when he kissed her more urgently, she kissed him back with everything she was, knowing a strange sense of sweet serenity. His hands slid down to settle at her hips and the beginnings of a restless urgency fired her senses. He pulled her between his legs, bending his back to mold her rounded figure to his body from shoulder to thigh. Susannah shuddered. He felt hard and demanding against her belly. Without giving herself time to weigh her actions, she pulled one of his big hands around to rest on her breast while she slipped her own smaller palm between them and cupped him in its warmth.

But then, while she was fully involved in responding to his desire, to the searching sweep of his tongue in her mouth, to the beginning movement of his thumb caressing her nipple, Whit suddenly, hastily, said, "This is no good." Releasing her abruptly, he turned and stared out at the ocean, sticking his hands into his back pockets and squaring his shoulders resolutely.

Susannah stood with her hands limp at her sides where they'd fallen. Her gaze fell without comprehension on the man who'd been kissing her senseless a moment ago. The set of Whit's broad shoulders looked tense and unyielding and his muscular legs were planted as though to withstand an assault by the devil himself. As the passion aroused by his demanding mouth drained away, her legs quivered, threatening to dump her on the sand.

This is no good. For whom? she wondered. Other than her daughter, Whit Montgomery was the best person to come into her life in a very long time. Painfully she thought back over all the shared moments of the past few weeks. She'd have sworn he was coming to care for her. But he'd clearly shown her just now that he didn't want her solace, her sympathy, or even the temporary respite her body offered.

Forcing her legs into action, she slowly turned away and started up the beach in the direction of the house. He didn't call her back.

The long, solitary walk back along the sand was the hardest thing she'd ever done. Knowing that Whit was hurting, every instinct within her screamed to comfort him. Acknowledging that her attempts would be rejected took a bit more time. Finally, as she left the soft, shifting sands and began to mount the steep incline, hard, harsh sobs tore through her, dry, wracking sobs that afforded no relief from the ache that invaded her heart.

Sinking down onto the narrow path, she wrapped her hands protectively around her swollen stomach, rocking back and forth. She cried for herself, for whatever quirk of fate decreed that she make mistake after mistake in her judgment of the men to whom she was attracted. She cried for the death of her dreams of a peace-filled life on a small Georgia island. She cried until at last the sounds of anguish faded, leaving her drained of everything but an immense weariness. Feeling as if she were a hundred years old, she hefted her walking stick and carefully began to pick her way back up the steep path to the house.

When she let herself into the kitchen, the room was dark save for a counter light burning near the sink.

"Where in hell have you been?"

Susannah knew that voice. She whirled as Whit switched on the overhead lights.

"I walked home." She winced at the raw, thick sound of her voice, but he didn't appear to notice.

Looming over her, he said "What were you thinking of? I've told you about the dangers here. No idiot walks around in the dark—" he indicated her clothing contemptuously "—in shorts and sandals. A snake would've had a great target if you hadn't been lucky!"

"I was careful," Susannah retorted, sitting down across from him. "I walked slowly and used my stick to clear the path."

Whit looked murderous. Although his voice never changed decibel, she felt the sting in every word. "Why were you out there so late? You left the beach in good time to get back to the house. I took the Jeep and I've been waiting here for fifteen minutes. What an idiotic trick!"

Susannah bit the inside of her lip so hard she tasted blood. The only thing that kept her from giving in to the anger that his derogation provoked was the knowledge that it *had* been stupid to get caught like that. Now he'd really be convinced she was no better than any other green city girl.

When Whit realized she wasn't going to argue with him, he made a sound of irritation deep in his throat. He spun and headed for the door. Then, as if an arrow had halted him in his path, he jerked to a stop. Swinging back around, he retraced his steps to the chair where Susannah still sat. He came nearer and nearer, bending until she could feel his breath hot on her cheek. One hard palm came out and covered the mound the baby made against her smock. She could feel the heat in every cell.

"Are you sure you're okay?" His tone was grudging, as if he hated to have to ask.

"The baby's fine," she replied stiffly, turning her head away. "I didn't harm the baby."

In a lightning-swift move she hadn't anticipated and never would have expected from the calm, controlled man she knew, the hand left her belly and grabbed her chin, forcing her head around. "I asked how *you* were," he grated. "If I want to know about the baby, I'll damn well ask."

Shaken, Susannah dropped her gaze from the fierce demand in his eyes. "I'm fine," she murmured. "Tired, but that's normal."

"Get some rest." It was a royal command.

When his gaze still pinned her in place, she realized he wanted an answer. "I will."

He looked at her for a moment longer, fingers gentler now on her chin. His thumb came up to brush across her lips a single time, then he released her. Before she could speak he banged out the back door and swung up into the Jeep.

Ten

The sound of the whining engine had faded into what was now full dark outside the big brick house when Hilda entered the kitchen. She gave a start when she saw Susannah sitting at the big kitchen table, then her gaze softened as she took in the evidence of recent tears. "You mopin' alone or can anybody join?"

"I'm all right. Just a case of the blues, I guess." Susannah hastily wiped her cheeks. She'd forgotten what a mess she must be. "Thank you for putting Becca to bed tonight. She's going to miss you when we leave."

For once, Hilda wasn't ready with a quick comeback. Faded brown eyes treated Susannah to a steady assessment that made her squirm. Finally she asked, "Have you decided to go, then?"

Susannah didn't know how to answer that. "We were only invited as temporary guests," she said softly.

Hilda snorted. Susannah realized with a pang that she was going to miss the woman's gruff mannerisms. "You're not interested in living on the island?"

What was the housekeeper getting at? "It's immaterial." Susannah made her voice firm. She wondered who she was trying to convince. "Whit made it very clear that this was only short-term. I'd planned to stay until the baby came, but after tonight..." Forgetting Hilda's presence, she sighed.

"You two had a fight."

Susannah came back to earth abruptly. "We did not have a fight." Her voice oozed wounded dignity. "I overstepped the bounds of Whit's hospitality." She stopped, thinking back over the scene on the beach. "I think."

"If you want to stay, don't let his ways drive you off."

That got Susannah's full attention. The reserve that was so much a part of her disintegrated at the look of compassion in the older woman's eyes. "Oh, Hilda, I don't know what to do. I want to stay. I've gotten accustomed to the island now and I can't imagine wanting to live anywhere else. But I'd go to New York City if that's where Whit wanted to live. I just want to be with him. But he doesn't feel the same."

"Who says?" Hilda was as blunt as ever. "I've never seen that boy look at a woman the way he looks at you."

"He's attracted to me because I'm the mother of his child."

"Hah! He must've been attracted to you before you had that baby in your belly."

Susannah flushed scarlet. "Well, maybe, but—"

"But nothing. I wouldn't have bet on you to stay twenty-four hours when you came here. I figured you'd be back on the mainland in a minute."

"Did you know Marguerite?"

Hilda's eyes flickered. It was the only sign of her surprise at the sudden change of topic. She nodded. "Yep."

Susannah waited. She'd pushed more than she'd ever have dared a day before.

"Woman was a witch," Hilda pronounced. "No red-blooded male could've withstood what she flaunted unless he was otherwise occupied. Whit never stood a chance, 'specially at the age of twenty-two. He wanted so bad to find somebody to share his dream...."

"His dream of establishing the loggerhead program?" Susannah prompted.

"No." Hilda waved a hand impatiently. "He already had the turtle volunteers coming, although it wasn't such a big operation then. No, I was talking about a family. Ever since he was a little kid, Whit's wanted a family. His no-account father couldn't stop his globe-trotting long enough to bother with a lonely child before he was killed, and as far as I know, Whit's never heard a word out of that selfish bitch who bore him and then ran off when he was little. Marguerite saw dollar signs when she looked at Whit and she set about acquiring them. For a while he thought she was going to be the mother of his children."

"But he didn't marry her." He'd told her that himself.

"Nope." Hilda's expression held relief.

"And there hasn't been anyone serious since then?"

Hilda raised one eyebrow. "Checking out the competition?"

Susannah blushed. "Just curious."

"In a pig's eye."

Whit crossed the flagstones the following morning as he came up from the hatchery for lunch. His attention was caught by the sight of the woman who knelt on the terrace, placing Becca's "treasures" into a plastic bucket, and his feet slowed. She finished as he reached her. Dusting her hands against the legs of her long shorts, she was maneuvering herself onto her knees when Whit stepped forward to offer her a hand.

Casting him a grateful yet wary look, Susannah used it to pull herself to her feet. "Thank you. You must have known some pregnant women in your lifetime. We appreciate all the help we can get.''

Without releasing her hand, Whit voiced what had been troubling him since he'd seen her levering herself to her feet. "Why don't you ask for help when you're having trouble? Even if I'm not around, Hilda or Axel would be glad to help you."

He'd startled her, he could tell.

She shrugged. "I'm used to doing things for myself. It didn't occur to me."

That stung. He wanted to shake her, to shout that he was there for her now, that he'd always be there to help her with anything she needed. But caution held back the impulsive words. He never shouted. And she had that look on her face again—the one he hated. That closed one that he couldn't read. Was he wrong about her? He'd thought she was beginning to care for him. She even seemed to love the island. He badly wanted to ask her to stay, but he couldn't bring himself to take the risk.

Shoving aside the disquieting feelings rolling through him, he carried her hand to his lips in a gallant gesture that surprised even himself. "What other things are difficult for pregnant ladies?"

Susannah made no move away from him. Her face softened and she appeared mesmerized by the way he brushed his lips back and forth over the back of her hand. "Um, soft seats," she said breathlessly.

"Soft seats?" His voice held a thread of amusement.

"Yeah." She warmed to her theme. "Soft, low seats are a prison sentence for a pregnant woman. You sit down on one and sink and sink and sink, and when you try to get out of it, you understand how a turtle flipped onto its back feels. Totally helpless."

Whit laughed. "What else?"

Susannah turned her hand so her fingers entwined with his. He didn't think she even realized she'd done it. "Tying shoes." Her words came faster and faster. "Shaving legs.

Getting out of a bathtub, sliding behind the wheel of the car." She paused, thinking again. "Getting out of bed."

The image her last phrase evoked in his mind was anything but amusing, and he could feel his body beginning to react to the memory of Susannah in his bed. He cleared his throat and his voice was husky as he said, "I can help with most of those—except maybe shaving your legs."

She laughed then, her eyes lighting up. "My hero." Then her face sobered. "Whit? Why did you...didn't you...want to kiss me last night?"

He stiffened. He knew he'd behaved like a jackass last night. He'd been so close to pulling her down in the sand and loving her...and he would have, if he hadn't suddenly had a moment's concern for her condition. That line of thinking had led to the reason for her pregnancy, and he'd suddenly resented her for making him so hot for her when she was planning to leave, when he still didn't know if she was going to shaft him with a legal suit over the child they'd created together.

"You're leaving soon," he said by way of explanation. His tone was almost challenging.

Susannah looked at him for a long moment before she gently pulled her hand away. "I am, aren't I?"

Having her confirm it made him feel worse than he'd felt since the day Ira had read him the stipulation in his grandfather's will. He stood unmoving, hands at his sides in defeat, as Susannah disappeared into the house.

In her room that afternoon, Susannah pulled the large suitcase out of the closet and laid it open on the bed. Tomorrow was the day Axel made his mainland run for supplies and she planned to be on the boat. It was unnecessary to continue imposing on Whit's hospitality when she was feeling so well.

Her step was heavy as she trekked to and from the dresser with armloads of the lightweight, casual clothing that were practically all she and Becca needed on the island. Until last night, she'd harbored a secret fantasy that Whit might actually be coming to care for her, that he'd ask her to marry him and raise their child—and Becca—on Turtle Island.

But his blatant rejection on the beach had cut to the bone. Today, the realization that he was only tolerating her presence, waiting for her to leave, abraded the wound in her heart even further.

This was the only sensible thing to do. He might not have said it in so many words, but he clearly wasn't interested in anything more than getting his baby in September. She flopped onto the bed with a dejected sigh, wishing she could give in to the urge to cry.

A knock on the other side of the door that led to Whit's room interrupted her self-pity. Her heart hadn't given up like her more rational mind had. It gave a great leap and began thumping madly as she raised her voice. "Come in."

"Hi." Whit stuck his head around the door. "Can I come in—what's this?"

He sounded puzzled and a frown spread across his features as she explained, "I'm packing. I thought Becca and I would go home when Axel goes for the mail tomorrow."

"Why now? Is it because of last night?" He crossed his arms and simply stood like a deeply rooted oak in the middle of the room, waiting for a response.

Susannah took a deep breath, aware as always of the strong pull of attraction. "No, it isn't because of last night."

"Are you still considering challenging the contract?"

She shook her head. At least she could give him that. "No. Seeing you with Becca has shown me what kind of father you'll be. I know you want this baby for itself, not because it's a way to keep the island."

Whit exhaled a deep, relieved breath. "I have to be honest. I don't know if I'd ever have done something like this if I had any other choice. But now..." His eyes warmed. "Now, even if I lost the island, I'd still want this baby."

"I know." Her voice was soft.

"So why are you leaving?" She'd forgotten how tenacious he could be when things didn't go his way.

"We've imposed on you long enough. I feel guilty making extra work for Hilda. The original reason for this argument was my health and I'm feeling fine now."

"I hoped you'd be happy here."

The words were an accusation to her ears. Did she detect a trace of... could it be disappointment? Wishful thinking, she reminded herself. Still, she couldn't lie to him about her feelings for his home. She wouldn't go away and let him believe she'd detested island life, even if she weren't the woman who would ultimately share it with him.

"I love it here," she told him honestly. "I thought I'd mind being cut off from everything, but—" she gestured out the window "—everything I need is right here." The urge to bare her soul rose up, nearly choking her and she fell silent for a minute while she battled for control of her treacherous tongue.

Whit jumped into the silence, ticking off on his tanned fingers reasons she should stay. "Then why not stay? I enjoy having you here. I'll miss walking on the beach with Becca and you, and I really have appreciated your help with the paperwork. You're much better at it than I am. Hilda and Axel would miss you, too. As for your health, I know you're feeling well, but isn't it easier here with all of us to help you with Becca? From everything I read, the last trimester is a time of decreasing energy for a pregnant woman. I'm afraid you'll wear yourself out if you're alone at home."

With a decisive nod, he crossed the room and began to take clothing out of her suitcase. When his arms were full, he turned and deposited the items in an empty dresser drawer. Susannah stepped in front of the suitcase as he approached it again.

"Oh, no, you don't!" She held up a hand in the manner of a stern cop directing traffic.

Whit feinted to the left and when she fell for it, he neatly dodged to her right, grabbing another handful of garments.

"Whit! Stop that! You're making a mess. I'll put it away myself."

He did stop then, regarding her over the top of a pile of practical bras and panties with a stretch panel distorting the front. "You mean, you'll stay?"

Susannah nodded. "I suppose so."

She took the underclothing from Whit's arms, stashing it quickly in a drawer as her cheeks grew hot. "Why did you come in here in the first place?"

Whit grinned. "Your graciousness overwhelms me." He hesitated, the teasing light in his eye fading. His manner grew diffident. "I was hoping to feel the baby move. Maybe this isn't a good time. I can come back later," he said, practically ushering himself out the door.

Susannah grabbed his arm, wanting to prolong any time alone with him despite the pain his presence engendered. "No, it's okay. Actually, this is a good time. He's almost always active in the late afternoon. Right now he's doing an aerobic workout in here." She patted her stomach as she drew him over to the bed. "Let's sit down for a minute."

She kept her voice and expression pleasant and light. He'd only asked her to stay so he could continue to play a part in his child's prenatal development, she felt sure. And loving him the way she did, she'd been unable to insist on leaving when he was so gently persuasive. She closed her eyes briefly when his big, rough hand slid over her stomach. Unexpected tears threatened. If only this could be real and lasting!

"You're right. He's really lively today." The wonder in Whit's tone was a source of both pain and pleasure. When had she begun to be glad she could give him this joy? And how could that be when it was killing her to think of giving up this baby? She savored the long, silent moments with both the precious one growing within her and the larger, equally beloved man at her side, touching the mound of his child with reverent fingers.

"I think the lump you feel here is his bottom," she said, directing Whit's hand toward a spot underneath her right breast. She hoped he couldn't feel her heart doing double-time at the thought of him sliding those callused fingers up to caress her nipple. Rushing on, she said, "And those are his feet you're feeling over there on the left. His hands are way down here—" She pointed just above her public bone. "When he waves his arms around, it tickles terribly."

"I bet." Whit's eyes twinkled. He was so close she could see the black ring circling his dark blue irises. "Susannah, I've been worrying a little bit about your labor and delivery. You're getting close enough to term that we should probably talk about arrangements."

What did he mean? Susannah hesitated. "What should we talk about? I'll have someone run me over to the hospital when I go into labor. Or if you're uncomfortable with that, I'll go home when I get close to my due date." A thought struck her. "I'll need to make plans for someone to keep Becca for a few days until I get home." She sighed. "I hate to ask Myrna to help again, but she's the only one I know—"

"Whoa, there." Whit gently tapped her stomach. "First I'd like you to stay right here until your time comes, if you want to. I'll take you to the hospital—I wouldn't miss it for the world. I'd like to have time right after the birth to bond with the baby anyhow, so I'd planned on coming over regardless."

When she only gazed at him, he passed a hand in front of her eyes as if he weren't sure she was attending. "Also, why can't Becca stay right here? She knows Hilda and Axel, and the routine will be familiar. She hasn't seen Myrna in a while and she might be afraid when we leave her. I hate for her to be uprooted needlessly."

He was looking at her expectantly. She said slowly, "That would be fine. Both about the hospital and about Becca. If Hilda agrees."

"*If* Hilda agrees? Are you kidding? She'll jump at the chance to have Becca all to herself for a few days."

Susannah was silent. Now that she'd agreed, the ramifications of her acceptance of Whit's plans were coming home. She'd have to somehow get Becca home again—for good—after her release from the hospital. That meant contact in one form or another with someone from the island. Not exactly what she'd prescribe at a time that was bound to be traumatic at best.

Although she hadn't told Whit, she was hoping to be released from the hospital the same day the baby was born. She'd been looking at maps just yesterday, trying to settle on a location to reconstruct her life with her daughter. If the labor went well, she'd been told she could be released as soon as four hours later. Then she planned to take Becca and simply disappear. She'd send for their furniture as soon as she'd found a place to live and a new job.

The job was going to be a problem. She didn't want to use Ira for a reference. This break had to be clean and complete. No one from her former life would be able to find her.

Not that they'd want to. These measures were to protect Becca, to keep her from ever learning at what price her life had been purchased. If they stayed in Glynn County, the risk of running into Whit was simply too great to take. And if anyone else ever found out about their bargain, she'd be the pariah of the county. She also had to protect herself. There was no way she could ever chance seeing Whit and their child after... after. Susannah knew her limitations. She'd fall apart if she permitted herself to think about the baby. If she ever saw it, she'd never be able to give it up. She wasn't even planning on holding it before she signed her child away.

Inside her body, the object of her anguished thoughts was increasing the pace of activity. It was as if the fetus recognized the sound of its father's voice. Whit was engrossed in murmuring to his child now, and the pleasant, husky sound washed over Susannah as she sat on the edge of her bed, caught between her misery and Whit's caressing hands.

"You know me, don't you?" he crooned. "I can't wait to meet you for the first time. You and I are going to have so much fun together." He smiled sheepishly as he caught Susannah's eye. "I feel like a little kid on Christmas Eve again. Except that this is much more exciting than opening presents ever was." In a lightning change of topic, he requested, "Tell me about your first labor."

Susannah's puzzlement showed in her eyes. "I already did."

"No." Whit's tone was indulgent. "I mean, the specifics. How you coped and how it felt and...just everything."

"I've never known a man who was interested in all the gory details before."

A fleeting shadow crossed his face and his eyes took on a faraway expression. "When I was involved with Marguerite, I used to dream about children. I think I was more in love with the idea of a family life than I was with her." Abruptly he snapped back to the present. Giving her one of those crooked, endearing grins she hadn't been able to resist since she'd met him, he wheedled, "Humor me. This is the closest I'll ever get to the real experience."

Susannah looked down to where his warm palm cupped her abdomen. His words strummed a sympathetic chord. "Becca was about five days early. I already told you about Steve's part in her birth—or should I say, the part he didn't play? I'd known when I got pregnant that he wouldn't go to childbirth classes, so I hadn't taken any. As a result, I was pitifully ignorant of what would actually happen once I went into labor. I stayed at home until the pains were five minutes apart, like they told me to. That was about five hours."

"And you were alone all that time?"

Susannah nodded. "Yes. I was getting overwhelmed by the pain and my imagination kept asking me, 'But how much worse is it going to get before it's over?' But I got lucky when I went to the hospital. The nursing staff was very kind. I was the only one in labor that day and a nurse stayed with me the whole time."

"How long?" Whit's voice was terse.

"About seven more hours. Twelve hours really wasn't bad for a first labor. The nurse who stayed with me was a godsend. She showed me how to breathe and forced me to follow her when I got frantic. When I was sick she was right there with me—"

"You must mean during transition."

Susannah stared at him. "You really have been reading up on this, haven't you? I never knew there was such a thing until I was in labor. This time, I'm determined not to be so naive. I've signed up for a four-week course the hospital offers expectant mothers."

"When is it?"

Susannah thought he was irritated because someone would have to make an extra trip into town. It was with a measure of smug relief that she told him, "It's offered on the same day Axel makes his run to the mainland. He said he didn't mind killing an extra hour if I wanted to attend."

"You're going alone?"

He sounded oddly wistful. A lightning bolt of daring shot through her, an idea so wildly impractical that her breath stopped in her chest. Did she...could she possibly give him such a gift? No. He wouldn't want to be bothered. She shook herself mentally. Old habits died hard—that was Steve Taylor talking.

The memory of how impatient he was for his child to make its appearance, of how eagerly he'd read anything to do with childbirth and infant development, stuck in her head. *This is the closest I'll ever get to the real experience.* Like an ornery burr under a saddle, it pricked at her mental denials until she blurted, "There's a different class—for couples who want to try natural childbirth." Breathless, she waited.

His eyes cut to hers once, a slash of hopeful blue. "For couples who are going to share the birth experience."

Seizing her courage in both hands, she voiced her thoughts. "If you'd like to, you could be my coach. You'd have to come to the classes with me, but then you could be there for the birth, to see the baby and hold it right away." She closed out the mental images her words evoked, concentrating on his face.

He controlled the look of profound, intense anticipation so quickly Susannah wasn't sure she'd even seen it when he responded. He hadn't moved, had barely breathed. "Are you sure you want to make an offer like that? I know this isn't going to be easy for you."

She held his gaze. "I'm sure."

Slowly, a smile broke across his features like the first kiss of golden sun on a shadowed dawn. "I'd be honored." He dropped the casual pose and his voice rose in excitement. "I'd be thrilled! When do we start?"

Rising from the bed, she crossed to her dresser and took a folded schedule from the top drawer. "Couples classes last eight weeks. They start next Wednesday! And they run from . . . oh, Whit, they're from seven to nine at night. I'm sorry. I know you can't leave the island at that time of day—"

"Want to bet?" He was grinning from ear to ear. "I hate to shatter your image of the dedicated biologist, but the birth of my child takes top priority. I'll shuffle the schedule so fast the others won't know what hit them."

Tonight was the night! Whit could feel anticipation thudding in his veins the minute he opened his eyes on Wednesday morning. He lay in the wide bed, looking at the ceiling, hardly daring to breathe until he came fully awake and could trust himself not to pad across the floor and throw open the door.

Mornings were tough. Hearing Susannah moving around on the other side of the door between their rooms was torture. He'd never considered himself oversexed in the past. Even the nearly celibate life-style he'd led in recent years hadn't been as much of a strain as living in the same house with her. He wondered if she'd be horrified if she knew what he'd like to do with her almost-seven-months-pregnant body. Or worse yet, what he'd like her to be doing to him. Somehow, remembering the way she'd responded to him the first time they'd come together and how wild she'd gone in his arms in the Island Habitat room, he couldn't believe she'd be too shocked. But he had to get his mind off those memories or his agitated state would be apparent to everyone at the breakfast table.

Besides, it wasn't only her body he wanted. What would it be like to lie with her cuddled next to him all night? To see those perfect features when he opened his eyes in the morning?

Susannah. He savored the flowing feminine sound of her name on his lips like a lovestruck adolescent. She'd fit into his life so easily that lately he hadn't been able to contain the fantasies. Apart from a few isolated moments when he'd caught a glimpse of sadness in her eyes, she seemed so happy that he could picture her a permanent part of Turtle Island, helping him with his research and raising their children. His mind had even worked out all the details. Susannah could finish her teaching degree so that when their children—he thought of Becca as his now—were of school age, she could tutor them right at home. At least until they were older and could go to boarding school as he'd done. Or maybe he'd alter his routine and make a mainland run every day of the week to take them to and from school. He simply couldn't envision sending Becca to live away from home as he'd done when he was a teenager.

But he couldn't afford to indulge in such thoughts. Susannah might appear to be contented right now, but when she was back in shape again, no longer heavy with child, surely the quiet routine on the island would get old. The restrictive social life would pall after a steady, year-in, year-out diet, and she'd be gone like his mother had.

No, better to let her go now and know that the choice had been his.

Eleven

Whit's palms were sweating. He carefully placed them on the knees of his trousers, shifting in the metal folding chair. His eyes were riveted to the scene being projected onto the movie screen at the front of the room.

It was the fourth childbirth class they'd attended. The film on the screen was a real-life birth.

He must've been crazy. The thought went around and around in his head like the bright arms of a pinwheel he'd bought for Becca. The woman in the movie was in the grip of a pain greater than anything he'd ever imagined. Her eyes were squeezed tightly shut and her face contorted. Her teeth bit viciously into her lower lip as her back arched off the bed.

He couldn't let Susannah do that. As his eyes slid sideways to her stomach, he acknowledged that it was too late to call it off. But how could he possibly help her? The techniques that had seemed so mysterious, and which the nurses assured him would help immeasurably, suddenly seemed

puny and ineffective. They must be joking. It was going to
take a lot more than a couple of silly breathing patterns to
get Susannah through this.

As if she read his mind, the object of his panicked
thoughts reached over and squeezed his hand. "Calm down.
I have confidence in you." Even through the disquiet, his
body recognized and responded to her touch, as always.
Again, he shifted in the chair. Turning his hand palm up, he
laced his fingers through hers. "Then you know something
I don't."

Her lips curved in a gentle smile. "You're going to be
great. You're the only man in here who memorized the
APGAR rating scale. Even I haven't figured out what it
means when I'm fifty-percent effaced, but you've got that,
too. And I bet no one else has a Lamaze bag with everything from tennis balls knotted into a tube sock to an en-
velope of change for the pay phone in it!"

She was depending on him. That thought alone kept him
from jumping to his feet and telling the nurses to forget it.
Susannah needed him. He knew he'd remember her trust in
him for the rest of his life.

August was hot and sticky. Susannah minded the heat
more than she'd ever thought possible. She rarely strayed
onto the beach except for her early morning walks now.
Even the exciting nightly forays of hatchling turtles couldn't
entice her out unless the sultry humidity let up.

Eight weeks to go. She'd forgotten what it was like to be
able to get out of bed without rolling, to sit with her legs
together, to jump out of a chair in one easy leap. Her bladder had shrunk to the size of a marble, if the frequency with
which she had to use the bathroom was any indication. She
waddled down the hallway to Becca's room after an afternoon nap. Another sign of her waning energy level—she no
longer resisted when Whit or Hilda suggested she take a nap.

"Mommy! I'm awake, Mommy!"

"Okay, okay, I'm coming." She entered the bedroom to find Becca sitting up in her bed clutching the white harp seal Whit had brought her in the hospital. "Hi, baby. Are you ready to get up?" The question was rhetorical.

As she changed Becca's diaper, she was struck by the thought that Becca would soon be out of diapers. She was already asking to sit on the potty during the day. Her baby was growing up.

A wave of depression gripped her as Becca ran out of the room ahead of her. She was sick to death of being pregnant, but she dreaded going into labor because then she'd lose this baby, too. She rubbed her swollen stomach gently. How could she do it? How could she walk away from her child at the time when the infant would need her most?

Everybody knew a baby needed its mother. She conveniently ignored the research studies she'd read in which fathers raised infants as competently as their feminine counterparts. Fathers couldn't breastfeed. She'd always believed so strongly in the value of mother's milk. It was just one more thing that was going to make it harder to leave her baby behind when she walked out of the hospital for the last time.

Dragging herself along in Becca's wake, she waddled into the hallway just in time to see her daughter vanish into an empty room down the hall. Susannah had never been in the room before, and she wondered who had opened it up.

"Becca, come back here," she called.

To her surprise, Whit's voice floated back to her. "It's all right. She's with me."

The room was a total shock. Pale blue carpet covered the floor. Two walls were a matching shade while the other two were papered in a pink and blue medley of bunnies and teddy bears gamboling across the walls. A border of bears and bunnies ran around all four walls next to the ceiling. Pink and blue checked curtains were tied back at the long windows. A low set of white shelves occupied one wall. On them were a number of books and toys that she recognized from Whit's various forays to the mainland. A white dresser with a changing pad atop it stood in one corner, and not far away was a tall chest of drawers. The pieces of a white crib were scattered over the floor and it looked as if Whit were having his customary luck reading directions. Becca was already rooting happily in a bag of screws.

"Hi!" Whit's voice was enthusiastic. "What do you think? It'll do for either a boy or a girl, won't it?"

Susannah was speechless. The misery that had been brewing within her coalesced into a big lump in her throat. Swallowing only made it worse. "It—it's fine," she managed to squeak.

Turning, she fled from the room, moving back to her own as fast as her ungainly body would move. When she got there, she realized she couldn't even throw herself across the bed for a good cry. It was the final straw, and she stood forlornly in the middle of the room while the tears streamed down her face.

"And pant, pant, pant, blow. Take a de-e-ep, cleansing breath . . . and get ready for another contraction!"

Susannah glared at Whit. "Oh, come on. Don't you think we've been at this long enough? You know the breathing patterns by heart, I know the breathing patterns by heart, everybody else on the island probably does, too!"

Whit smiled and extended a hand to help her into a sitting position. Becca had been in bed for more than an hour and they'd been practicing since then. When she had struggled up, he went around behind her and began to massage her back. "I just want to be prepared." His voice was surprisingly gentle.

Conversely, his tone irritated Susannah. She'd been particularly testy for weeks now, and Whit had grown more soothing and patient by the day. It made Susannah long for a rip-roaring fight. "Well, I don't care if I'm prepared or not," she snapped. "And you shouldn't either. After all, my role in this is of little importance. You'll get your baby even if I scream for twenty hours."

Whit's hands stilled on her back. He was silent for so long, she thought he wasn't going to answer her. Then he got to his feet. Looking down at her, he said with quiet force, "I know this isn't easy for you. How do you think I feel about myself, seeing what I'm doing to you?"

She didn't have a ready response to that, and he spun on his heel and strode out of the room. A minute later Susannah heard the kitchen door slam. She dropped her head, ashamed. The ever-present tears welled up again and splashed down her cheeks, dripping onto the huge mound distorting her now nonexistent waist. Only six more weeks to go. The countdown preyed on her mind, spoiling her pleasure in every waking minute of the day. Even her sleep was disturbed by shadowy dreams in which she begged a white-clad nurse to let her hold her baby, but the nurse turned and left the room while Susannah struggled from the bed and ran to the door, only to find it locked.

Regardless of her inner turmoil, she had no right to be angry with Whit. He'd been patient and kind, doing everything possible to make her life easier. He'd entertained Becca far more than Susannah suspected he really had time to, even taking her out with him during the day sometimes.

If only he could lo—no! A thousand times a day she caught herself wishing for the moon. She'd given him every brazen signal she could to let him know she was attracted to him. She'd gone out of her way to be sure he knew she loved the island, too. He probably even knew she was in love with him. If he wanted her, he'd have said so by now. He was so determined not to let another woman leave him that he wouldn't chance a relationship.

And she couldn't change that. In six weeks, she'd be walking away from Whit forever.

Whit and their baby.

"Hilda! I need a bandage. Old turtle came about a millimeter from taking off my thumb." The kitchen door slammed behind Whit three weeks later.

Hilda shook her head as she bustled into the kitchen. "You need a keeper," she muttered as she briskly wrapped the nipped digit.

Whit snickered. "You applying for the job?"

"You gotta be kidding. Besides, I know a certain silver-blond beauty who's already in line for the position."

"She's only temporary, Hilda," he said quietly.

Hilda raised an eyebrow. "What's that supposed to mean? The woman's condition might be temporary, but the responsibilities that go with it are going to last a long time."

"I can't ask her to marry me. We both knew going into this that it was simply a business proposition—hey! Ouch!"

Hilda picked up the scissors and snipped at an end of gauze she'd yanked too tight. "Maybe it didn't start out as a passionate love affair, but there's no reason it can't become one."

Whit couldn't suppress a smirk. "I never said it wasn't passionate."

The housekeeper ignored the comment. "That's even more reason to keep her. Sex is an important part of marriage."

"Come on, Hilda," Whit said wearily. "You know how women feel about bright lights and action. Susannah wouldn't last any longer than my mother did on Turtle Island."

"That's the stupidest logic I've ever heard! She's lasted so far, hasn't she? And from what I see, she seems to love it. Marguerite never pretended to like the island, and your mother didn't, either. Besides, what am I?"

"A very special woman," he said fondly.

The older woman blinked. Her mouth twitched into a soft smile before she returned to the discussion. "Do you love her?"

Whit didn't even hesitate. "Yeah. I love her." It was an exhilarating feeling to finally admit it.

"Then tell her and give her the chance to decide."

Could he do it? Hilda was right. Susannah had adapted unbelievably well to island routine. She didn't seem to be a woman who craved the glitter of mainland nightlife, nor even the daily conveniences that living in a city offered. She hadn't been appalled or repelled by the natural dangers inherent to his home. Instead, she'd sensibly learned all the precautions that everyone else followed, and stuck to them.

He considered what life would be like when Susannah had gone and he was alone again. Of course, he wouldn't really be alone. He'd be raising her child. He'd never considered the implications of that before, but it would be a different version of hell, seeing her features combined with his on a miniature, wanting to share all the exciting "firsts" with her. He'd grown used to seeing her face light up when he came through the door at night. She certainly wasn't immune to his touch. Could she love him? Enough to make her life on the island he called home?

He had to do it. If he didn't take the risk, he'd always wonder. It scared him stiff. He'd probably have a hell of a time forcing the words out, but he had to ask her to marry him and stay on the island.

Two mornings later Susannah waddled slowly along the beach, keeping an eye on Becca as the little girl danced in and out of the frothy breakers running up the sand.

Whit watched her coming, noting the bent head, the slump of her shoulders. Both of her hands massaged her lower back as she walked. He wished the next three weeks would pass quickly, for her sake. He'd never realized what a tremendous strain these final days of pregnancy were on a woman's reserves of energy and emotional stability. He'd been as attentive and helpful as he could, but still she appeared to be getting more depressed as the days passed. As he stared, she put a hand to her cheek, wiping it outward in a careless gesture.

Was she crying? He felt a stab of guilt. No wonder she was depressed. She still thought she was going to be giving up her child in a matter of weeks. He knew exactly why he'd

been delaying for the past two days. He was scared. Gutless
Montgomery, that was him. He was so afraid she was going
to turn him down that he'd been making up excuses right
and left to keep himself from begging her to marry him.
Wanting to keep her baby, and marrying a relative stranger
to do so, were two different propositions entirely. Stranger.
His mouth quirked into a small smile as he decided that
what they'd shared in the past months hardly permitted
them to call each other "stranger."

Steeling himself, he walked toward her. This was it. He'd
ask her for a date. With some time alone, perhaps they
could talk openly about the future. "Susannah?"

"Hi, Whit." Her voice was uncharacteristically husky.
She wiped her cheeks again furtively before she turned to
face him.

Becca was getting too far away, and Whit took Susannah's hand, drawing her down the beach. As always, the feel
of her soft skin against his gave him a rush of pleasure.
"Becca, wait for us," he shouted. When he looked down at
Susannah, she was studying him indulgently. "You're going to be such a good father," she said. "You react like a
parent without even being aware of it."

"Thanks for the vote of confidence. I confess I get more
nervous as the time gets closer." She smiled, and he was encouraged to continue. "Susannah . . . would you have dinner with me tonight?" When she looked up at him,
uncomprehending, he elaborated. "We could go over to the
mainland and have a nice meal." He thought that was a
stroke of genius. It would be an act of compromise, to show
her that if she was willing to marry him, he'd suffer a certain amount of the social whirl.

She looked blank, her violet eyes wide. "I thought you
hated stuff like that."

"I don't love it, but you look like you could use some
cheering up. Besides, I have something to talk to you
about."

"Can't we talk here?"

"Here? Now?" Did she mean right here, as in, on the beach? "Don't you want to go out to dinner?" Women, he thought. Who could ever guess what they were thinking?

She shook her head and his heart sank, but then she smiled again. "Not now. I'd rather have dinner here. If you want me to, I could ask Hilda to set up our meal on the terrace after Becca's in bed. It would be beautiful under the stars. I'd prefer that to a meal in a restaurant."

Had he died and gone to heaven? He couldn't have ordered a more perfect evening? Relief—and anticipation— heated his voice to a timbre that brought pink to her cheeks. "That's a wonderful idea. I'll meet you on the terrace at eight."

Susannah opened the bathroom door and walked into her bedroom. She stopped in surprise as Hilda whirled away from the closet.

"Goodness sakes! You scared me." The housekeeper put a hand to her heart.

"I didn't know you were here. What's the matter?" Hilda was holding the pink shorts and flowered maternity top Susannah had laid out to wear as if they smelled of three-day-old shrimp.

"Nothing's the matter...exactly," Hilda hedged. "Is this what you're wearing tonight?"

"Unless it has a hole in it, yes."

The older woman sighed. "You hardly ever get a chance to wear any of your pretty dresses. Why don't you put one on tonight? After all, you won't have to worry about Becca getting it all dirty. I already fed her and gave her a bath. She's waiting for you to kiss her good-night."

Susannah stared at Hilda until the housekeeper dropped her gaze. "I don't guess you'd have any particular dress in mind." The words were loaded with sarcasm, but Hilda perked right up.

"Well, yes. You could wear that pretty blue one with the white lacy jacket. I hung it on the closet door in case you felt like dressing up."

Hilda pointed, and reluctantly Susannah turned. "That pretty blue one" just happened to be the dressiest thing she owned. She still didn't know why she'd packed it all those months ago when she'd come to Turtle Island to stay. She'd worn it when she was pregnant with Becca, as she had all her maternity things. But it had only been worn a handful of times and still looked like new. She'd probably never wear it again after this pregnancy ended. The thought increased her melancholy.

She exhaled slowly. "All right. I guess I could wear it." Why not? She was too depressed to argue with Hilda, who obviously had her mind set on seeing Susannah in the dress.

Standing in front of the mirror after bidding her daughter good-night, she had to admit that whatever Hilda's motives, her instincts had been right. The dress was an ice-blue confection of layers of chiffon that swirled around her enlarged figure in a decidedly feminine manner. The top was daring, boasting two thin spaghetti straps that held up the sweetheart-cut bodice. With the lushness Mother Nature bestowed upon an expectant mother, it was more revealing than anything Susannah would normally have worn. Thankfully the sheer, lacy jacket with its short sleeves and single pearl button, hid her ample bosom enough that she felt comfortable.

She felt pretty. Better than she had in days. Whit would probably think she was crazy for dressing like this, but she didn't even care. Mentally thumbing her nose at his imaginary reaction, she left her room and went downstairs. The dining room was dark and she went through it to the French doors. The sun was setting over the ocean. She paused a moment, engrossed in watching the fiery orange ball descend to the horizon in a blaze of pinks and golds. When a pair of large hands settled on her shoulders, she started in surprise.

A masculine voice growled in her ear. "Stick 'em up."

"Oh, please, sir, have mercy." She forced a note of mock fear into her own tones to cover the breathlessness that always assailed her when he touched her. Butterflies that had nothing to do with pregnancy leaped to life in her abdomen.

"Never." The robber laughed, a deep sound whose heat warmed her neck, making her shiver involuntarily. "Give me all your gold or pay the price."

"But, sir, I'm only a simple maid. I have no gold."

Whit turned her to face him. "Then, wench, you'll have to forfeit a satisfactory substitute." Without giving her a chance to draw a breath, he pulled her into his arms. She was dazed by the speed with which the game had turned into something more, and when his dark head bent and his hot mouth covered her own, she couldn't offer even the smallest protest.

He kissed her thoroughly, plunging his tongue boldly into her mouth, holding her against him with one arm while the other slid up to caress her breast through the thin fabric of her bodice. Because of the protrusion of her belly, he held her at an angle, his own length pressed against her hip and side. As their mouth play grew more intense, she could feel him hardening against her hip.

When she hung limp and breathless in his arms, he slowly diminished the urgency of the kiss. His hands went around her, holding her lightly as he withdrew his mouth. Rubbing his nose back and forth against hers, he pronounced, "That was better than gold."

Susannah was silent. What was going on? Why had he deliberately kissed her like that? The possible answers to that made her head swim. When she didn't speak, he took her hand and opened the French doors. "I suppose we'd better get out there and do justice to Hilda's meal or she'll never do this for us again."

She'll never do this for us again anyway. Less than three weeks from now I'll be gone. The thought erased any pleasure she was feeling from the heated kiss.

Then Whit ushered her onto the terrace and her attention was caught by the scene before her. She temporarily forgot her black mood as she gaped. "Hilda, this is beautiful!"

The housekeeper was busy setting up a tray stand near the patio table. The umbrella had been removed and a white tablecloth covered the glass surface, rippling in graceful folds around the edges. A bowl of roses had been arranged in the center of the table, and flanking it were two small candelabra with white tapers already burning brightly. The firelight struck sparks off the platinum-edged china and crystal and the silver flatware at each of the two place settings.

As Whit led Susannah to the table, Hilda turned and winked at her. "Don't thank me," she said, but there was no bite to her words. "I just followed orders." And she turned and bustled off toward the kitchen.

Behind her, Whit said, "May I seat you?" and she whirled. She knew her heart was in her eyes, but she didn't try to temper her reaction. "Oh, Whit, thank you. This is the loveliest thing anyone's ever done for me."

For the first time she really looked at him—and sent a silent prayer of thanks to Hilda for goading her into wearing the blue dress. It had been weeks since she'd seen him in anything but casual clothing. Even when they'd attended the childbirth classes, he'd worn shorts. She'd caught a number of the other women in the room eyeing the way the garments fit his tightly muscled buttocks from time to time.

Tonight he'd donned a pair of navy dress slacks and a long-sleeved striped dress shirt. A navy patterned silk tie and fine leather loafers completed the transformation.

He was scanning her garb with equally open appreciation. Heat ran through her veins as his gaze lingered at her breasts. "You look absolutely beautiful."

"Thank you." She fingered her dress. "For a cow."

"Stop denigrating yourself. I happen to like you pregnant. You glow."

"I ... glow?"

"Yeah." He ran a finger around his collar. "I'm terrible at compliments. Let's eat."

He indicated her chair and helped her slide into it. Before he took his own seat across from her, he took an icy bottle of champagne from a silver bucket strategically placed near the table and popped the cork. Filling two fluted champagne glasses with sparkling golden liquid, he handed one to Susannah. "I don't think one small glass will hurt the baby."

Seating himself, he lifted his glass. When she did the same, he proclaimed, "To new beginnings."

Susannah echoed the words. "To new beginnings." But as their glasses chimed in a traditional toast, her heart protested in pain. Her new beginning was going to be missing some very vital things in it.

Dinner was a culinary event extraordinaire. Hilda pulled out all the stops with dish after succulent dish. Whit seemed lighthearted and carefree and Susannah made an effort to hold up her end of the conversation as they discussed Becca's health, the childbirth classes, and the loggerhead program.

By the time a delicate sorbet arrived for dessert, the sun had set, the moon had risen and they'd run out of conversational lifelines. Finally, in the face of her silence, Whit pushed back his chair. "Shall we walk a little?"

"I'm so full I'll probably roll." Carefully, Susannah arose. Her hands went automatically to her back. The nagging backache that had plagued her all day was worse than ever tonight. *Only three more weeks.*

Whit moved behind her. "Back hurt?"

"Uh-huh." Susannah let her head drop forward as he massaged the sore area. "Oh, thank you a thousand times. That feels wonderful."

He used his strong hands to soothe her for long moments, then took her hand and pulled her over to the white marble railing that bounded the terrace. "Look at that," he whispered, turning her toward the water. The moon made a silver-white path across the midnight water, and Susannah had to admit it was a beautiful sight. She was far more aware of the way Whit moved up behind her, pressing his body close against her, bringing his big hands to rest on the upper swell of her gravid belly. "Isn't this nice?" he murmured in her ear.

His breath stirred the curls at her temple and Susannah could barely concentrate on what he'd asked her. What *was* he up to tonight? "Very nice," she agreed breathlessly.

"We could—"

But she never found out what he was going to suggest they do because one of the young female students came up from the beach, stopping short at the edge of the terrace when she saw the pair of them standing in the moonlight. "Oops, sorry," she said in a cheery tone. "I'm going in for the antiseptic. Cut my toe on a piece of shell." Then she looked beyond them to the candle-lit table with the remains of their meal. "Oh, that's sweet," she said ingenuously. "A romantic meal before the stork descends. I guess the time's approaching, huh?"

Susannah felt as if she were frozen. But Whit must've managed a nod or some indication of assent, because the girl looked satisfied. Then she focused her wide brown eyes directly on Susannah. "What are you hoping for this time? Another girl to play dolls with Becca would be nice, but a little boy would be so cute—" The student gave a gasp of surprise when Susannah pulled away from Whit and ran headlong for the house, moving as fast as her bulk would permit.

Twelve

————

Fifteen minutes later Susannah turned off the shower. Her back felt marginally better than it had most of the evening, but her eyes were puffy and swollen from the violent bout of tears she had unleashed in the safety of the bathroom. Dully, she stepped from the enclosure and toweled herself, removing the shower cap from her head.

Another surge of self-pity swamped her and an unexpected sob tore from her throat. She thought she was all cried out but apparently she'd been wrong. Fresh tears cascaded down her cheeks. She'd discarded her clothing in the bedroom; blindly she reached for the knob of the bathroom door.

She'd taken three steps toward the dresser where her nightclothes were before she realized Whit stood beside her bed.

She froze, misery forgotten in the crushing embarrassment of having him see her nude. And not just nude—enormous and ungainly to boot.

Whit looked as shocked as she felt. His gaze traveled over her from the tip of her tousled curls down over the huge swell of her belly...and further. Flame leaped in his eyes. He moved, a great shark steadily stalking a hapless sea creature, and she was finally released from her strange malaise.

"Get out," she cried.

He was beside her by then. "I can't," he muttered. "It's too late." Then his hot, hard hands came down on her shoulders, pulling her bareness against him at the same time his mouth descended onto hers.

There was nothing tentative about his kiss. He was a pirate staking a claim, as bold as he'd been in front of the French doors earlier in the evening. His tongue thrust between her lips, demanding passion, licking, plunging, sliding over the inner surfaces. His mouth tasted of champagne and of the sorbet they'd consumed. He bowed his body to accommodate her new shape. Against her nakedness, the fabric of his shirt felt strangely, coarsely exciting and her nipples contracted almost painfully in response to the unfamiliar stimulation. The hands that gripped her shoulders gentled, slipping down over her damp back, stroking the sides of her rounded waist and exploring the globes of her bottom, coming around to explore the soft down between her legs and linger at the mound of her belly before palming her engorged breasts. She shouldn't want this, couldn't allow this. Her mind gave her reeling senses commands in vain. Her body knew who was petting it, knew what it wanted. It wanted Whit.

"Mmm, sweet." He tore his lips from hers and breathed the words over the sensitive skin of her neck as he nipped and kissed his way down her throat. His tongue trailed along her skin, leaving a path of liquid fire in its wake. "I've dreamed of touching you for so long. Like...this." As his marauding mouth closed over a nipple, Susannah gasped aloud. The drawing, pulling sensations plucked chords deep inside her, creating a begging need deep between her legs.

Somewhere in the silent house, a clock began to bong out
the hour. In her room, the only sounds were of her rasping
breath and the greedy noises of his suckling. Restlessly, she
moved against him. Her hands came up to urge his mouth
even more fully over her and her fingers plunged into the
rich textures of his hair. She stroked the line of his jaw, savoring the silky skin as he drew on her breast. He must've
shaved right before their dinner. Sliding her palms down,
she encountered the heavy muscle of his strong neck and
shoulders camouflaged by the dress shirt he still wore,
though the tie had been discarded and the top button torn
open.

"Let me touch you," she gasped, reaching under his chin
to tug futilely at the stubborn buttons.

"Uh-uh." He shook his head as he let her nipple slide
from his mouth, crooning to her. "This time I want to touch
you, kiss you everywhere. Let me love you." He slipped one
arm behind her back, the other under her knees. Effort-
lessly, he lifted her into his arms, much as he'd done so
many months ago.

"I'm too heavy," she objected.

His voice was warm and rich with amusement. "You said
that before."

"And this time I mean it! Put me down."

"Whatever mi'lady desires." She felt the soft give of the
mattress under her back as he laid her gently on the bed that
had belonged to his mother. The sheets were crisp and cool
under her and the scent of line-dried freshness rose to en-
velope them.

He didn't give her a chance to think about what she was
doing before he was beside her, claiming her breast with his
hungry mouth again, throwing one leg over hers and bending it at the knee to nestle intimately between her thighs. The
gentle nudging at the apex of her legs stole her breath and
set a wave of liquid fire racing through her to dampen the
silver curls against which he was pressing.

She arched upward, moaning and straining.

"Sh-h-h." He soothed her heated flesh with long strokes of his hands, running his palms repeatedly over the bulge of his child distending her belly. "You're so beautiful."

"This isn't fair. Take off your clothes, too." She fumbled with the fastenings of his pants, but he pulled her hands away with gentle but inexorable force.

"No, love. We can't . . . I can't take off my clothes."

"We can," she insisted, jerking her hands away and renewing her attack. "This time I want you inside me when you—"

Her words were lost under the force of his kiss. "Are you sure? Is it safe?"

Lord, how she loved him. If this were all she could have, then she wanted a night, one last night, to remember for the rest of her life. She'd keep her promise, never try to see her baby, but she wasn't strong enough to deny herself this. She took his face between her hands. "I'm sure. It's safe. *Please*, Whit. Don't make me beg."

He rolled away from her so fast she was left with her hands hanging in the air. So he didn't want her after all—

And then he was back, his glorious nakedness sliding against her, heating her skin everywhere that he touched. She could feel the rigid proof of his desire for her leaping and throbbing against her thigh. Instinctively she rolled onto her back, trying to pull him with her. He resisted with an ease she could only envy. "No. I don't want to hurt you." Grasping her wrists, he slid to his back and drew her atop him.

Eagerly, she parted her thighs and sat astride him, feeling the shaft of his manhood snug beneath her. He was magnificent. His skin was flushed and rosy beneath his deep tan, his cheeks ruddy with arousal. His bronzed shoulders gleamed. She slid back until he was exposed, then her hands tenderly enclosed him within their small cradle. Up and down, she caressed him between her palms, until his breathing was labored and he was groaning with each stroke. He fit his palms to her heavy breasts, rotating them over the turgid peaks. The enticing movements made her long for more. Unable to wait, she lifted herself to her knees and guided him into her.

When the slick, velvety tip of his engorged flesh made contact with the soft feminine folds above him, Whit grasped her hips, holding her motionless for a instant. "Ahh... I've wanted you for so long."

Susannah ran her hands over his chest, up to his shoulders and back down across the rigid muscle of his abdomen. It rippled under her touch. Fascinated, she repeated the action. Under her fingers, his flesh was firm and silky, roughened here and there by springy curls, pearled with droplets of perspiration. She shifted her hips above him, rocking languidly, and a grimace of pleasure crossed his face. His eyes narrowed and he smiled at her. "Want to play, do you?" His voice was so rough and gritty, she had to strain to understand his words. Slowly he delved deeper by tiny increments, making a place for himself within her.

She could feel a rush of moisture between her legs at the erotic contact as her body prepared for the act of love. Catching him off-guard, she suddenly bent her knees and sank down, embedding him to the hilt in her tight warmth. He filled her completely, large and alive and a gasp of surprised pleasure escaped her when he flexed his buttocks and forced himself even more deeply into the chalice of her body.

He apparently mistook her gasp for pain because an alarmed expression registered in his gaze and he automatically began to withdraw from her. "What's wrong?"

Susannah tightened her inner muscles around him, giving him an unintended caress. "Nothing. You feel...so good."

He relaxed beneath her, allowing his hardened flesh to return to its snug nest. "So do you, love. So do you."

The endearment warmed her, though she knew it was nothing more than an expression of his desire. She resumed the rocking motion, her breath rushing in and out, feeling a great force gathering within her abdomen, a clenched fist of need growing tauter, tenser, tighter. Whit's fingers clenched her hips in a vise of iron. Beneath her, he began his own rhythmic thrust and retreat, slamming into her grinding pelvis with sweet intent, stimulating her starved senses. With the added sensuality produced by her pregnancy, Susannah could endure only moments of his heavy assault until her body exploded, jerking and throbbing over, around him. Experiencing her intimate release was too much for Whit, and beneath her his body suddenly doubled its frantic rhythm until, with a shout of completion, his body followed hers into climax, spewing jets of his seed deep into her receptive warmth in a vain attempt to do what it successfully had done before.

As the bucking roll of his torso subsided beneath Susannah, she became aware of her fatigue. She was suddenly so lethargic she could barely summon the energy to move. She couldn't fall forward so she moved off him and lay at his side. Immediately, he turned and slipped his arms around her, possessively cradling her. One big hand repeatedly stroked the stretched flesh over her belly, where for once the baby lay quiescent.

"Do you think we frightened him?" The question in her ear carried a note of tender amusement.

She responded equally gently. "I doubt it. Mother Nature fashioned his little home for maximum protection. He probably just thought he was on his first roller coaster ride."

Whit laughed and squeezed her carefully. "You are some amazing lady."

Susannah couldn't reply until after she'd completed an enormous yawn. "Right now, I'm some tired lady."

His arms tightened around her. "Go to sleep, love. We can talk when you wake up." The words carried a special promise that soothed her, but she was simply too exhausted to pursue it. Her eyes closed and she slept.

The ache in her back made her restless. She lost count of the number of times she turned over, a beached whale

heaving her bulk from side to side in a futile attempt to get
more comfortable. Each time she did, Whit was there, rubbing her back, cuddling her close. Despite the discomfort,
she was content.

Whit opened his eyes. The bedside clock read 5:45. He
could barely see the digital display over the top of Susannah's head where she was snuggled deep into his arms
against the heat of his body. One of his hands spread protectively over the mound of his child; he could feel occasional rhythmic contractions harden her belly. Susannah
had explained that these "false alarms" didn't hurt and were
quite common in a second pregnancy, but he was still
amazed that she could sleep through the sensations.

Speaking of sensations . . . he could feel the stirring flesh
of his loins rising to salute the memories of last night. Being nestled into the crease of Susannah's buttocks wasn't
going to help. Resolutely he forced his mind away from the
delightful recollections. She hadn't slept well at all. He'd
never really thought about how it must be to sleep with a
basketball in your belly. Clearly, it wasn't a lot of fun. He'd
done what little he could, kicking himself all the while for
not being more aware of her needs before. He could tell her
back hurt. If only he'd—

"Ohmigod!" Susannah sat bolt upright in the bed. Before he could react, she'd rolled out and fled toward the
bathroom.

"Susannah!" he yelled, leaping up and running across the
room after her. "What's the matter?"

She'd slammed the bathroom door, and when he rattled
the locked knob, she called, "Wait!"

"What's wrong?" He was frantic. The feel of dampness
under his foot made him glance down. He could see a dark
trail from her side of the bed to the bathroom. He was about
to break down the door when she answered him.

"My water broke."

"Your water broke?" Then it hit him. *"Your water broke!"* His voice turned accusing. "You said it was safe."

"The doctor said it was safe," she hollered back. Then her voice gentled. "Calm down. I'm thirty-seven weeks along. Everything's probably fine."

"Susannah, the baby isn't due for three more weeks. You can't have it yet."

There was a strangled laugh from her side of the door. "Okay, Whit. You tell the doctor that."

Dr. Bradley! "I've got to call Dr. Bradley." He wheeled and ran toward the door.

"Whit?"

"What?" He ran back.

"Could you bring me a pair of panties and my robe?"

He moved to obey. The simple act calmed him and as he handed the requested items through the door, he asked her, "Don't you want clothes?"

"I want to take a shower first."

A shower? "Susannah, we have to get to the hospital! You don't have time to take a shower."

The bathroom door opened a crack and her lovely face peered out. It was set in lines of determination. "I am *not* going to the hospital until I've had a shower. Now why don't you go take one, too? And eat some breakfast. You're going to need it." She winked at him and the door closed.

He nearly choked on his frustration. "But we might not have time!"

"We'll have time." The shower began to run. "Call Dr. Bradley and tell him my water broke but I'm only having a few mild contractions. We'll be at the hospital in about an hour."

An hour. One hour. Surely his child wouldn't be born that fast. If he hurried her, they could make it in forty minutes.

"If you could just fill out this form for me, Mr. Taylor—"

"Can't you see she's in labor? I'll do it later."

"I've already called an orderly to take her on up to the birthing unit. Now why don't you sit down and fill this out?" Behind him, Susannah walked back and forth, back and forth, rubbing her belly, totally focused on a contraction.

The nurse withdrew her hand. "You're doing nicely, Mrs. Taylor. Five centimeters dilated."

Only five centimeters! And she had to go clear to ten. From his position by her head, Whit watched Susannah adjust her gown and climb down. She seemed to be more comfortable on her feet—walking gave her something to concentrate on throughout each contraction. So far, he hadn't felt she really needed him.

Just then, she turned and flashed him a wan smile. "This is so much different than my first labor experience . . . so much more intense. Thank you for being here."

"And pant-pant-pant, blo-o-ow. That's my girl, exhale all the way."

Susannah was on the birthing bed now. The contractions had become so intense she felt more in control reclining slightly. She clung to Whit's hand so hard he knew he'd have bruises later. Her eyes were fixed on his face as her focal point while he talked her through the contraction that tightened her body.

"And take a deep, cleansing breath." She obeyed, but already he could feel her body beginning another contraction where his hand rested on her abdomen for that very reason. "Get ready. Here comes another one."

"No-o-o-o! I can't take this. Whit, I need something for the pain. . . ." Her voice trailed away as he got down right in her face and forced her to follow his lead and breathe.

The nurse who'd attended them all the way heard her last words. Expertly, she raised Susannah's gown and at the surcease of the contraction, she checked her progress

"Ahh!" Her tone held a wealth of satisfaction. "You're doing great, honey. It won't be long now. You just keep on breathing. Don't let her push," she instructed Whit. "I'll go get the doctor."

Whit wiped Susannah's brow with a cool cloth and offered her ice chips when the next contraction ended. "We're almost there, love, almost there."

Almost there. Images hit him with the force of a fist in the gut. Soon he'd be holding his child!

"Okay, little lady, are you ready to push?" Dr. Bradley seated himself at the foot of the birthing bed between Susannah's raised knees. Susannah grunted with the effort to hold back. "Let's get this show on the road, then," the obstetrician pronounced. Almost as an afterthought, he threw the next phrase at Whit. "You better get down here—you'll miss all the action."

Immediately, Whit moved to the foot of the bed. He hoped Susannah wouldn't feel self-conscious, but he could've saved the worry. It was humbling to watch her in the role women have played since the dawn of time, life-giver, Earth Mother, perpetuator of the race.

"Bear down *now,*" Dr. Bradley instructed her. Whit watched in awed fascination as a crown of dark hair appeared in the perfect circle. Mere minutes later, the infant slid from its warm cocoon into Dr. Bradley's waiting hands. Tears ran unashamedly down Whit's cheeks as he watched the doctor and nurses do all the things he'd been warned to expect with the tiny person he'd helped to create.

"What is it?" Susannah's tone was curiously lifeless.

"A girl!" His jubilation spilled over into his voice. "And she has dark hair! The doctor says she's small but doing fine."

"Are you disappointed?" She sounded apprehensive.

"Disappointed? Are you crazy? She's beautiful!" He moved to her side and leaned over, giving her a tender kiss before his eyes were drawn back to the sight of his daughter. His voice grew husky. "That was the most wonderful thing that's ever happened in my life. Thank you so much for letting me share it.''

Susannah waved a limp hand dismissively.

"Who wants to hold her first?" piped the cheery nurse.

"Her father," Susannah got out.

The doctor returned to Susannah, and in a little while, the entire birth process was complete. Dr. Bradley congratulated them and left the room. All the nurses left except the one who'd been with them from the start. "Just one more question, Mrs. Taylor," the vivacious nurse said. "Are you planning to breastfeed?"

"No," said Susannah.

"Yes," said Whit. He was holding his new daughter wrapped carefully in both arms as if he were afraid to move with her.

The nurse raised an eyebrow. "Well, which is it?"

"I can't—" Susannah began miserably.

"Yes, you can," Whit returned. "Trust me, love."

The nurse, apparently sensing that something momentous was occurring, waved a bottle at Susannah. "I'll leave this just in case. You two can stay in here for an hour. Buzz us when you're ready to go to your room, or if anything unusual occurs. If you want to try to breastfeed, go right ahead. I see from your chart that you've done it before." And she whisked out the door.

Whit approached the bed. "Want to see our little miracle?" His eyes shone with a warm light.

"Whit..." Susannah swallowed and tried again. She couldn't think of any easy answer. Four hours of labor, while a short stint by any standards, had drained her. All she wanted was to get as far away from Whit and the baby as she could so she could begin to accept the unacceptable. "I can't hold her—or look at her. I could never let her go if I did."

Over her protests, Whit dodged her defensive maneuvers and laid his precious bundle in her arms. Then he wiped away the tears that fell from her cheeks onto the swaddling blanket. "You don't have to, love. Forget about that stupid contract. I could never take your child away from you." He put a finger over her lips when she attempted to speak. "The turtle project will find some other way to survive if I can't finance it. At least, that's a risk I'm willing to take. This little lady needs you."

Susannah raised her eyes to his, and in them he saw the beginnings of an incredulous joy. "Oh, Whit, thank you," she cried. "But she'll always be your daughter, too. We'll work something out, I promise. It'll be just like we're divorced and working out custody. I'll make sure she can stay on the island with you some of the time, maybe when she's not in school." Almost frantically, she seized his hand and kissed it before rushing on. "I know you value your privacy and I promise I won't intrude. I'll just—"

"Susannah." Whit placed his hand over her mouth to stop the flow of words. Then he laid his other hand over hers where they clasped the infant to her breast. "If that's what you want, we'll work it out." He paused and took a deep breath, starkly aware that his whole future hinged on his next words and how she received them. "But I've had a dream almost since the first time you came to the island. I love you. I've been trying to get those words out for days, but it suddenly seems easier after what we've accomplished together here. Would you consider marrying me and living out on the island?" He sucked in another breath and slowly exhaled it, knowing that without her, the island, his whole life, meant nothing. "If you get island blues like my mother did, I'm willing to try living on the mainland with our family."

A stunned silence followed his words. Susannah's mouth worked, but she couldn't make her numbed throat produce any sound. She began to cry—again. When would she ever regain control of her wayward emotions? Then his words began to penetrate. Whit loved her. He wanted to marry her. He wanted her…thoughts tumbled over each other. "What about Becca?"

He looked sober. "Becca…could I adopt her? She's mine in all the ways that matter in my eyes."

It was too much. Susannah took his hand again and cradled it to her cheek. "I love you," she confessed. "I've loved you for so long, but I was determined to uphold my end of our bargain. Of course I'll marry you and allow you to adopt Becca—but on one condition."

Whit looked apprehensive when she hesitated, and she savored the sweetness of the moment. "You'll have to promise me that you'll never try to make me leave Turtle Island. I've come to love it and I don't think I could be happy anywhere else."

As her words sank in, an expression of joy lit Whit's deep blue eyes with a marvelous inner fire. Leaning forward, he clutched her to him convulsively. "Oh, how I love you," he whispered against her hair. "And you." He touched his daughter's cheek with a gentle finger. "Have you thought about a name for her?"

Susannah shook her head with a rueful smile. "Hardly. I thought that was going to be your job, remember?"

"We'll do it together," he pronounced. Then a flame of heat leaped in his eyes. "Seems to me we're pretty good when we decide to work together."

Susannah blushed. "You weren't so sure of that at six o'clock this morning."

Whit smoothed her hair back from her face. "But I was at midnight last night." He sighed. "Six weeks, right? Six long, cold weeks before we can—"

"Whit Montgomery! You're going to have to watch your language in front of our daughters," Susannah chided him with a tender smile.

He laughed, pulling her to him for a kiss. Between them, their daughter began to squawk indignantly, and he stepped back with a delighted laugh. "Sorry, little one. Your mother and I were just sealing a lifetime contract."

*   *   *   *   *

SPRING FANCY

Three bachelors, footloose and fancy-free... until now!

Spring into romance with three fabulous fancies by three of Silhouette's hottest authors:

ANNETTE BROADRICK
LASS SMALL
KASEY MICHAELS

When spring fancy strikes, no man is immune!

Look for this exciting new short-story collection in March at your favorite retail outlet.

Only from

Silhouette®

where passion lives.

NORA ROBERTS

Love has a language all its own, and for centuries flowers have symbolized love's finest expression. Discover the language of flowers—and love—in this romantic collection of 48 favorite books by bestselling author Nora Roberts.

Two titles are available each month at your favorite retail outlet.

In March, look for:

The Art of Deception, Volume #27
Untamed, Volume #28

In April, look for:

Dual Image, Volume #29
Second Nature, Volume #30

Collect all 48 titles
and become fluent in

THE LANGUAGE of LOVE

Silhouette®

SILHOUETTE® *Desire*

HAWK'S WAY

HAWK'S WAY—where the Whitelaws of Texas run free till passion brands their hearts. A hot new series from Joan Johnston!

Look for the first of a long line of Texan adventures, beginning in April with THE RANCHER AND THE RUNAWAY BRIDE (D #779), as Tate Whitelaw battles her bossy brothers—and a sexy rancher.

Next, in May, Faron Whitelaw meets his match in THE COWBOY AND THE PRINCESS (D #785).

Finally, in June, Garth Whitelaw shows you just how hot the summer can get in THE WRANGLER AND THE RICH GIRL (D #791).

Join the Whitelaws as they saunter about HAWK'S WAY looking for their perfect mates... only from Silhouette Desire!

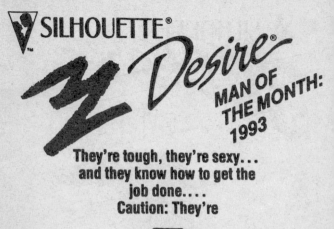

Silhouette Books
is proud to present
our best authors,
their best books...
and the best in
your reading pleasure!

Throughout 1993, look for exciting books
by these top names in contemporary
romance:

CATHERINE COULTER—
Aftershocks in February

FERN MICHAELS—
Nightstar in March

DIANA PALMER—
Heather's Song in March

ELIZABETH LOWELL
Love Song for a Raven in April

SANDRA BROWN
(previously published under
the pseudonym Erin St. Claire)—
Led Astray in April

LINDA HOWARD—
All That Glitters in May

When it comes to passion,
we wrote the book.

Silhouette®

BOBT1RR